in

Fate's Reins

by Debra Chapoton

book 1

in the *Hearts Unbridled* series

Copyright © 2024 by Debra Chapoton

All rights reserved.

ISBN: 9798864394458

Imprint: Independently published

No part of this book may be reproduced in any form or by any electronic or mechanical means, including information storage and retrieval systems, without written permission from the author, except for the use of brief quotations in a book review.

Books by Debra Chapoton

Unbridled Hearts series:
(Cowboy Romance)
Tangled in Fate's Reins
Rodeo Romance
A Cowboy's Promise
Heartstrings and Horseshoes
Kisses at Sundown

Loved by a Highlander series:
(Scottish Romance)
The Highlander's Secret Princess
The Highlander's English Maiden
The Highlander's Hidden Castle
The Highlander's Heart of Stone
The Highlander's Forbidden Love

Second Chance Teacher Romance series written under pen name
Marlisa Kriscott (Christian themes):
Aaron After School
Sonia's Secret Someone
Melanie's Match
School's Out
Summer School
The Spanish Tutor
A Novel Thing

Christian Non-fiction:
Guided Prayer Journal for Women
Crossing the Scriptures
35 Lessons from the Book of Psalms
Prayer Journal and Bible Study (general)
Prayer Journal and Bible Study in the Gospels
Teens in the Bible
Moms in the Bible
Animals in the Bible
Old Testament Lessons in the Bible
New Testament Lessons in the Bible

Christian Fiction:

Love Contained
Sheltered
The Guardian's Diary
Exodia
Out of Exodia
Spell of the Shadow Dragon
Curse of the Winter Dragon

Young Adult Novels:
A Soul's Kiss
Edge of Escape
Exodia
Out of Exodia
Here Without A Trace
Sheltered
Spell of the Shadow Dragon
Curse of the Winter Dragon
The Girl in the Time Machine
The Guardian's Diary
The Time Bender
The Time Ender
The Time Pacer
The Time Stopper
To Die Upon a Kiss
A Fault of Graves

Children's Books:
The Secret in the Hidden Cave
Mystery's Grave
Bullies and Bears
A Tick in Time
Bigfoot Day, Ninja Night
Nick Bazebahl and Forbidden Tunnels
Nick Bazebahl and the Cartoon Tunnels
Nick Bazebahl and the Fake Witch Tunnels
Nick Bazebahl and the Mining Tunnels
Nick Bazebahl and the Red Tunnels

Nick Bazebahl and the Wormhole Tunnels
Inspirational Bible Verse Coloring Book
ABC Learn to Read Coloring Book
ABC Learn to Read Spanish Coloring Book
Stained Glass Window Coloring Book
Naughty Cat Dotted Grid Notebook
Cute Puppy Graph Paper Notebook
Easy Sudoku for Kids
101 Mandalas Coloring Book
150 Mandalas Coloring Book
Whimsical Cat Mandalas Coloring Book

Non-Fiction:
Brain Power Puzzles (11 volumes)
Building a Log Home in Under a Year
200 Creative Writing Prompts
400 Creative Writing Prompts
Advanced Creative Writing Prompts
Beyond Creative Writing Prompts
300 Plus Teacher Hacks and Tips
How to Blend Families
How to Help Your Child Succeed in School
How to Teach a Foreign Language

Early Readers
THE KINDNESS PARADE, THE CARING KIDS: Spreading Kindness Everywhere
THE COLORS OF FRIENDSHIP: THE CARING KIDS, Embracing Diversity
BELIEVE IN YOURSELF, THE CARING KIDS: Building Self Esteem
FRIENDS WITH FUR AND FEATHERS: THE CARING KIDS, Animal Friends
CELEBRATIONS ALL YEAR ROUND: THE CARING KIDS: Our Special Days
FEELINGS IN FULL COLOR: THE CARING KIDS: A Guide To Feelings

Chapter 1

THE SUN DIPPED low on the horizon, casting a warm orange glow across the vast expanse of the Montana prairie. Jet Armstrong stood at the edge of the ranch, his weathered cowboy hat shielding his steel-blue eyes from the last rays of the day. His gaze was fixed on the grazing horses in the distance, a sight that stirred a sense of calm within him.

Two years of combat had etched lines of experience onto his rugged face, but they hadn't dulled the fire in his eyes. He had seen the brutality of war, felt the adrenaline surge through his veins as bullets whizzed past, and known the camaraderie of brothers in arms. But amid the chaos, he had also lost a limb, a part of himself that he thought defined who he was.

"Suck it up," Jet said to himself as he turned and walked toward the ranch buildings, ignoring the pain in order to stride without a limp. He had made a decision, a small but important step toward reclaiming his life. Despite the lingering doubt that clouded his heart, he was determined to find a way to heal, both physically and emotionally.

That determination led him to the Double Horseshoe Ranch, a place renowned for its prized horses, large cattle herds, and the breathtaking beauty of the surrounding landscape. A fresh start was what he needed, away from the haunting memories that plagued his dreams. He had heard about a stable hand position, a simple task of mucking out stables and caring for the horses. Jet had once been a rider, a true cowboy who could handle any horse thrown his way, but that was before the explosion that had taken his leg and his confidence.

Walking into the ranch office, Jet was greeted by a stout woman with a warm smile. "You must be Jet," she said, extending a hand. "I'm Martha, the owner. We spoke on the phone. I'm glad to have you on board."

Jet shook her hand firmly, a hint of gratitude in his eyes. "Thank you, ma'am."

"Your reputation precedes you," Martha continued. "I heard you've got a way with horses. And I believe every ranch needs a man with a heart for animals."

He offered a faint smile, appreciating her kind words. "I'll do my best, ma'am."

In the months that followed, Jet immersed himself in the rhythm of ranch life. He rose before dawn, the crisp air biting at his skin as he went about his chores. The stables were a refuge of sorts, a place where the smell of hay and the soft nickering of horses offered a soothing balm to his restless soul. Each time he brushed a horse's coat or looked into their soulful eyes, a sense of connection washed over him. It was a connection he had thought he'd lost forever. He ached to throw on a saddle, mount up, and ride across the great expanses ... but ... no ... it was one thing to grit his teeth against the shooting pains and quite another to endure complete failure. And failure it would be if he couldn't feel the stirrup, if he couldn't grip with knees, if he couldn't balance in the saddle.

Beneath the surface of his newfound routine, the remnants of war still lingered. Nights were often filled with nightmares, vivid memories of explosions and screams that echoed in his mind. He had taken the step of seeking help, attending physical therapy to regain his balance and control, and visiting a kindly psychologist, Dr. Langdon, who helped him tread the deep waters of post-traumatic stress disorder.

One evening, as the sun painted the sky in shades of pink and gold, Jet finished his chores and walked toward the ranch house. He glanced back at the stable doors, contemplating the fear that had kept him from riding again. His heart yearned for the freedom he had once known atop a horse, but the fear of falling and losing control held him back.

As he entered the cozy living room of the ranch house, the scent of a hearty meal greeted him. He joined the other ranch hands around the table, laughter and jokes filling the air. It was a stark contrast to the silence of his own thoughts.

After dinner, Jet retreated to his small room in the bunkhouse. He sat on the edge of his bed, his gaze fixed on the faded photograph of him riding a wild stallion, a fearless grin on his face. That version of himself felt like a distant memory, a relic of a time before the world had changed, his family had left Montana, and he'd had to grow up.

With a sigh, he reached for his journal and began to write, the words flowing from his pen as if they had been waiting for release.

Another day on the ranch, and I'm still here, still fighting. The horses remind me of what I've lost, and yet, they also remind me of the strength that must still be here inside me.

As the ink dried on the page, a knock at the door startled him. "Come in," he called.

The door opened, and Martha stood there, her German Shepherd companion at her side and a knowing smile on her face. "Mind if I have a seat, Jet?"

He nodded, setting the journal aside. "Of course, ma'am." The dog came over, sniffed him, and settled at his feet. "How ya doin', Duke?" He rubbed the old dog's ears.

Martha took a chair across from him and folded her hands on the table. "I've been watching you these last few months, Jet, and I can tell you're wrestling with something. Horses have a way of bringing out our truths, don't they?"

He studied her, surprised by her perceptiveness. "Yes, they do."

"Tomorrow," she said, her eyes steady, "I want you to join me for a ride. It's time to face that fear, even if it's just one step at a time."

Jet's heart raced, a clash of anticipation and anxiety growing within him. But in Martha's gaze, he saw a glimmer of faith, a belief that he could conquer his demons. And for the first time in a long while, a spark of hope ignited in his soul. He didn't want to disappoint this kindly woman. "Please, ma'am, not yet. I need a little more time."

Duke raised his eyes and gave him a mournful look.

Chapter 2

THE EARLY MORNING sun filtered through the curtains of Dawn Dupree's small apartment, casting a soft golden glow across the room. She stirred in her bed, the sheets tangled around her, as the muffled sound of her alarm clock buzzed on the nightstand. With a sigh, she reached over and silenced it, knowing that another day of her mundane job awaited her. She was behind in her rent and the landlord was giving her only three more days to pay up or she'd be out on the street.

Dawn possessed an understated beauty that didn't always capture men's attention. Her blonde hair flowed in soft waves, and a sprinkle of freckles graced her otherwise clear complexion. Her warm hazel eyes held both curiosity and vulnerability.

She'd spent years working at a job she despised. The pay wasn't quite good enough, though her boss kept dangling raises and bonuses in front of her. They never materialized, but the silly hope that one day he'd make good on his promises was the only reason she tolerated it for so long. She had debts to pay off, student loans that hung over her head like a dark cloud. But each day that she stepped into the office, she felt a piece of her soul wither away.

Her boss, Richard Stanton, a leering and condescending man, had made her time there even more unbearable. His incessant comments and unwelcome advances had driven her to the brink of her patience. Yet, she had endured it all, reminding herself that this job was a means to an end.

But this morning her tolerance reached its limit. Richard demanded that she stay late to complete a task not in her job description. Fueled by unexpected courage, Dawn refused, standing up to him for the first time. The confrontation was heated, words exchanged like daggers, until he finally spat out the words that left her stunned.

"You're fired, Dupree. You think you can challenge me? Good luck finding another job with your attitude. And good luck getting your last paycheck. I had to replace your old computer and I'm charging you for the new one."

Her heart pounded as she gathered her belongings and walked out of the office, the weight of his words heavy on her shoulders. She had no backup plan, no other job lined up, and her financial situation felt more dire than ever.

As the job-hunting days turned into a week, Dawn's frustration grew. The job market was tough, and with her credentials, she wasn't in high demand. Prospects remained scarce, and the looming pressure of her debts seemed insurmountable. Her landlord had given her a few extra days out of sympathy, but he knocked on her door Friday night to demand she be out by Monday.

On Sunday morning, feeling defeated and lost, she walked into the small church she attended. The warm embrace of the congregation offered some comfort, but it was Martha's presence that truly lifted her spirits. Martha was a woman of wisdom and grace, someone who had always believed in Dawn's potential.

After the service, Dawn approached Martha with a heavy heart. "Martha, I don't know what to do or who to talk to. I can't tell my sister; she doubled up on classes and, … oh, it's all so useless. I've lost my job, I have to be out of my apartment by tomorrow, I have nowhere to go, and I'm drowning in debt."

Martha placed a hand on Dawn's shoulder. "Don't worry, dear. Sometimes, life takes unexpected turns for a reason. Keep your faith and stay strong. Something will come your way. In fact, if you're willing, I have a temporary position that will hold you over for a while. And it comes with a room—not an apartment, but a nice room in the ranch house. My chef—cook, really—is taking eight weeks off to be with his wife and new baby. If you can boil potatoes, roast chicken, and bake bread you'd be a God-send, honestly. I just can't do it all by myself."

Martha radiated a motherly presence as comforting as a well-worn quilt. Her graying hair, styled in a classic bun, seemed appropriate for ranch life. Kind lines framed her eyes. Though she looked nothing like how Dawn remembered her own mother, she was definitely giving off those maternal vibes that made Dawn feel that everything would work out. It was an easy decision for her to make.

One day later, Dawn drove through the gates of the Double Horseshoe Ranch, her car packed with her clothes and a few possessions. Martha's offer of a temporary position cooking for the ranch hands would give her the cushion she needed as she kept looking for a position in the corporate world. Playing housemother to a bunch of ranch hands wasn't her dream job, but the opportunity to escape her suffocating circumstances was a lifeline she couldn't ignore.

As she drove onto the ranch, the sight of the sprawling landscape took her breath away. Horses grazed peacefully, and the fresh air carried the scent of hay and earth. A sense of calm settled over her, like she had stumbled upon a haven of rest despite her turmoil.

Martha greeted her with a warm smile, embracing her as only an old Christian friend could. "Dawn, I'm so glad you accepted. We could use some good meals around here."

Dawn returned the smile, appreciation swelling in her heart. "Thank you, Martha. This means a lot to me. But I'm warning you … I'm not the best cook." She laughed and so did Martha.

"Neither am I, but thankfully these boys—I should say men—eat anything."

In the days that followed, Dawn immersed herself in her new role. The ranch kitchen became her happy place, where she could pour her heart into her cooking and create delicious meals that brought smiles to the faces of the ranch hands. There were seven of them and she'd begun to think of herself as Snow White. She had always liked to bake and enjoyed the creativity of designing meals and especially desserts. The atmosphere was worlds apart from her previous job, and she felt a new sense of purpose. Everyone seemed to accept her, even the dog, who curled up on the kitchen rug and kept on eye out for the scraps she generously tossed him.

On the third evening, as the sun dipped below the horizon, Dawn settled herself in the living room of the ranch house. She glanced out the window and spotted one of the men sitting on the porch, lost in thought. There was something about him, an air of quiet strength mixed with vulnerability, that drew her attention. She hadn't learned all the men's names yet. She'd heard a few: Pete and Chase and Chris and Corey and … hmm, she couldn't remember them all.

Martha joined her, following her gaze. "That's Jet Armstrong. He's been through a lot."

Dawn turned her attention to Martha, curious. "What happened?" Jet, she thought. Tall with a strong, athletic build. His hair, kissed by the sun, fell in windswept waves that framed a face underscored by grit.

"He's a war veteran, lost a limb during combat," Martha explained. "And lost his spirit. But he's finding his way back, with the horses and the ranch."

Dawn felt a pang of empathy for Jet. She understood the struggle to find a way forward after facing life-altering challenges. But there was something in Jet's eyes, a fire that spoke of resilience, that captivated her.

Over the next two weeks, as Dawn cooked a variety of meals and navigated her way around the ranch kitchen, she crossed paths with Jet more often. They exchanged small smiles and casual conversations, each encounter leaving a lingering sense of connection. She ignored his occasional limp and he ignored anything she burned.

One evening, after cleaning up the kitchen and still hearing the dining room abuzz with a post-supper card game that Martha encouraged, Dawn stepped out onto the porch, the cool breeze soothing her tired muscles. She found Jet there, gazing up at the stars. Their eyes met, and at that moment, something passed between them.

"Beautiful night," Jet said, his voice soft.

Dawn nodded, her heart racing. "Yes, it is."

"Sit with me?" He motioned to the rocker Martha usually sat in and he lowered himself into a second chair. The evening breeze rustled through the nearby aspen trees.

Jet took a deep breath and looked at Dawn. "So, how are you finding life here at Double Horseshoe Ranch, Dawn?"

Dawn glanced at the darkened scenery surrounding them, a small smile tugging at her lips. "It's quite a change from my old life. I love the serenity of this place."

Jet agreed. "Yeah, it's a world away from the chaos I've seen. I've spent a lot of time in places that didn't have a patch of green for miles. Makes you appreciate this, you know?"

"You've been to some rough places?"

Jet's eyes clouded for a moment. "Yeah, I've seen my fair share of … ugliness. But it's different here. The beauty, the peace, it helps replace the bad memories."

"It sounds like you've been through a lot, Jet."

He offered a small, grateful smile. "We all carry our burdens. What about you? You left a job in the city, right?"

Dawn nodded, her gaze drifting to the stars twinkling in the night sky. "More like I got let go. But … I was stuck in a job that was draining the life out of me, taking care of … some personal stuff … and trying to make ends meet. I didn't know I needed this big of a change. Getting fired was a Godsend. This place, it feels like a fresh start."

Jet studied her, his voice gentle. "Sometimes a fresh start is exactly what we need. We're lucky to have found this place."

Debra Chapoton

Chapter 3

JET ARMSTRONG'S FATHER had experienced a rather sudden advance in wealth and power. The Armstrong name grew in the business world, the success of his new company unparalleled. Jet had been expected to give up his interest in ranching and riding and take over the fledgling company at some point. He had majored in business and marketing, and minored in finance. He was a natural at whatever he tried. He could have slipped off his cowboy boots and gone into the professional world as easily as slipping on a pair of men's Ferragamos. It was expected of him. It was also expected that he'd marry his childhood friend—a Montana girl from a good family—and uphold the family's newfound and prestigious reputation.

But life had a way of veering off the expected path. The call of duty had led him to enlist in the military, leaving behind a promise he never thought he would break. He had been engaged to a woman who had vowed to wait for him, a promise that had carried him through the darkest days of combat. But when he returned home, changed by the war and missing a limb, he found her unwilling to accept him as he now was: incomplete. He didn't blame her, but the loss of his fiancée echoed in the chambers of his broken heart.

Betrayed and disillusioned, Jet made a choice that defied his family's expectations. He turned his back on the business

Tangled in Fate's Reins

empire that awaited him and sought a new purpose at the Double Horseshoe Ranch. Here, he found solace in the companionship of the horses, the friendship of the ranch hands, and the kindness of Martha. After a while, he realized he'd never loved his fiancée the way one should love a woman.

Unknown to everyone including Martha, Jet had been quietly supporting the ranch with his own funds, determined to keep it afloat. The ranch was more than just a place of healing for him; it was a mission, a second chance at life that he refused to let slip through his fingers. And what better way to use those college degrees?

One tranquil August afternoon, as the sun climbed higher in the sky, Martha approached Jet, her expression serious. "Jet, can I talk to you? You're the only one of the men who seems to take this job as more than just a paycheck. You love this place, too, don't you?"

He turned to face her, his heart tightening in his chest. Had she discovered his financial meddling? "Of course. Why do you ask, Martha?"

She sighed, her gaze fixed on the horizon. "The ranch is facing a challenge, a big one. The state is planning to build a highway, and they want it to cut right through our land. They're offering to compensate us, but you know how much this place means to me. It's all I have left of my husband."

Jet's heart sank at the news. The ranch had become his haven, his place of redemption. He couldn't imagine it being replaced by a cold expanse of asphalt and concrete. "Is there any way to fight this, legally?"

Martha's expression grew somber. "It's possible, but it would be a long and spendy battle in court. And even then, there are no guarantees. I'd have to sell off half the cattle or half the land to get the money to hire a lawyer."

A heavy silence settled between them as the seriousness of the situation sank in. Jet's mind raced, searching for a solution, a way to protect the ranch he had come to love. It was more than just a place to heal; it was a symbol of second chances, of redemption, and the place he felt most comfortable in hiding from the corporate world his father kept urging him to enter. If money was all she needed, then maybe he had a way to help.

"You're not alone in this, Martha," Jet said softly. "I'll help you make the best decision for the ranch. I think I can find an investor, someone who might take a ten percent interest in your profits … or something like that."

Martha nodded and bit her lip. She swiped a hand across her wet eyes.

Jet's resolve strengthened. He had faced battles before, both on the battlefield and within himself. The stakes were high, but he refused to let the ranch be lost to the march of progress without a fight. For a lot less than ten percent, he'd make it his fight, too.

"Let'em buck. We'll beat this."

Tangled in Fate's Reins

Chapter 4

THE RANCH KITCHEN hummed with activity as the warm aroma of dinner filled the air. Dawn moved around the stove, a sense of purpose driving her. Cooking had become a personal fulfillment, a way to express herself now that she was resigned to never working in an office again. She had found contentment in preparing meals for the ranch hands; the way their faces lit up at the taste of her creations warmed her heart. She must have inherited some gastronomic inventiveness from her mother; it made her smile to think so.

As the dinner bell rang, Pete and Jet and Chris and the others gathered around the long wooden table, their voices mixing with laughter and the clinking of cutlery. Dawn watched from the corner of the kitchen, a satisfied smile tugging at her lips. It was a feeling of accomplishment she hadn't experienced in Richard Stanton's dreary office.

Just as she was about to step forward with a platter of steaming roasted vegetables, Jet Armstrong's voice cut through the chatter. "Dawn, might I make a small suggestion about that dish you're about to set down?"

Dawn's heart skipped a beat, her grip on the platter tightening. She turned to face him, her brows furrowing. "What do you mean, suggestion?" The word had triggered a memory of her old boss criticizing her. Duke, trotting out from the kitchen, picked up on her mood and barked.

Jet's gaze met hers, his blue eyes locking onto her with a calm intensity. "Well, just a tip, really. I've noticed that sometimes these roasted veggies don't—"

"Don't what? Don't measure up to your standards?" Dawn's cheeks flushed, her pride stinging. She had spent hours perfecting her dishes, and here was Jet, a mere stable hand, a man she thought she'd made an affable connection with, offering culinary advice. Her voice came out sharper than intended. "Are they overcooked? Undercooked? Not enough flavor? Thanks for the input, but I think I know how to cook my own dishes."

The room grew quiet, and Dawn could feel the eyes of the ranch hands on her. She imagined whispered comments and a few not-quite-lewd suggestions drifting her way. Her imagination added to her discomfort. She had wanted to prove herself, to earn respect for her new-found skills, and now she felt like she was on display for judgment.

And now she was ashamed that a few words from a nice guy could set her off like this.

But before she could retreat further into her shell, Jet's voice broke through the tension. "Well, I was just going to say that I wished you'd make twice as much, because sometimes these roasted vegetables don't make it around the table. Chris hogs more than his share." The men agreed and laughed, phrases like *so delicious* and *yeah, make more* reaching her ears.

Dawn's lips twitched, a trace of amusement breaking through her defenses. She eyed him, skepticism mingling with a flicker of something else. Had he changed what he was going to say or had he originally meant to compliment her? "So, you're asking for more vegetables?"

"He is," Chris dug into the dish as soon as she set it down. "He's got a hollow leg, you know."

Tangled in Fate's Reins

Jet's lips puckered then suddenly curled into a mischievous grin aimed at Chris. "My good leg isn't hollow and the other one is made of titanium and can kick your butt any day of the week."

Laughter erupted from the ranch hands, and even Dawn couldn't hold back a chuckle. She shook her head, a smile finally breaking through. "All right, cowboys, eat up."

As the tension dissipated, Martha entered with a flourish, carrying Dawn's dessert which stole everyone's attention. The chocolate layer cake was a masterpiece, each layer stacked high and topped with a rich ganache that glistened in the light. The ranch hands' eyes widened, and even Dawn couldn't help but admire her latest creation.

"Behold," Martha announced with a grin, "the *pièce de résistance* of the evening: a triple-layer chocolate cake, guaranteed to melt your worries away. And, Chris, you'll be served last."

The men erupted into cheers and applause, their conversation shifting to more lighthearted topics as they eagerly anticipated dessert. Jet caught Dawn's eye, and his playful smile told her that he hadn't meant to slight her cooking.

Later, as Martha cut slices of cake, she steered the conversation toward a more serious topic. "Now, as much as we enjoy the pleasures of good food, there's a matter we must discuss. The ranch is facing a challenge. We've been offered compensation to make way for a freeway, but it means giving up this land I hold dear and of course, you'd all have to be let go. I wanted all of you to be in on my decision. What do you think? Do we sell or do we fight?"

It was unanimous: fight.

"Good. I hoped you'd feel that way. I've received a generous offer to fund a court fight, but it comes with a strange request. Our anonymous benefactor wants at least one of you men to find a woman to marry within the next six months."

The room grew quiet once again, the curious condition on the advance of funds was a strange factor. Jet's gaze met Dawn's, and she quickly looked away. The ranch was more than just a place to work or eat; it was a shared refuge for all of them: Dawn because she lost her job, Jet because he couldn't face the commercial world, Chris because his family had lost their spread, and on and on with the other cowboys. They each had a story about why they'd come to Double Horseshoe Ranch, and why they would never leave. It was truly a haven that had brought them all together. But to arrange a marriage to get monetary support to keep the ranch? What was that all about?

As the chocolate layer cake disappeared from plates and conversation centered on mail-order brides and available sisters, Jet and Dawn avoided eying the other.

The taste of the chocolate cake stayed on their tongues. The thought of marriage lingered on their minds.

Chapter 5

TWO NIGHTS LATER Dawn stood in the ranch kitchen, her hands deftly working as she prepared ingredients for the evening meal. The savory aroma of herbs and spices filled the air, and she focused on the rhythm of her tasks, the now-familiar comfort of cooking grounding her.

As she sliced extra vegetables with precision, her concentration was broken by a presence nearby. She glanced up to find Jet Armstrong leaning casually against the counter, his dazzling blue eyes fixed on her. The intensity of his gaze sent a shiver down her spine, making her fingers falter briefly.

"Dinner smells incredible, Miss Dupree," he remarked, his voice as smooth as honey, sending ripples of warmth through her.

Dawn cleared her throat, pushing aside the unexpected jolt his presence caused. "Thank you."

He didn't move; his protracted gaze ignited a spark of something within her. She had never been on the receiving end of such intense attention, and it left her feeling both flustered and intrigued. She couldn't ignore the zings of attraction pinging all over her body.

"You know," he began, breaking the silence, "I've learned a thing or two about cooking. Would you mind if I offer a suggestion?"

Dawn's heart skipped a beat. She remembered the last time he had offered advice, and she was determined not to let his words ruffle her this time. "*Another* suggestion? Hmm, well, I'm always open to new ideas."

His lips curled into a playful smile, a glint of sly glee in his eyes. "Well, the last cook—he was good—but he didn't have much imagination. Sometimes his dishes could have used a little more ... dazzle."

Dawn raised an eyebrow, her lips twitching into a smirk. "Dazzle? An interesting word for you to use."

Jet chuckled, his gaze locked onto hers. "Yes, dazzle. A pinch of unexpected flavor, a dash of surprise, something to make a good dish stand out from the rest. The last cook was, shall we say, a bit routine. You're much better, but ... mm, I'm craving dazzle."

She felt a blend of annoyance and pleasure, unsure whether to take him seriously or not. "And how would you suggest I add this 'dazzle'?"

He leaned in slightly, his gaze never leaving hers. "Well, it's all about embracing the unexpected. Mixing flavors you wouldn't normally pair, adding a dash of spice where no one would expect it. You get the idea."

Dawn's lips parted, her irritation melting away into curiosity. "You're saying I should be more adventurous?"

He nodded, his eyes holding hers in a steady gaze. "Exactly. Take a risk, let your creativity flow, and who knows what culinary wonders you might create?"

She found herself drawn into his gaze, his words weaving a subtle spell around her. Despite her initial reservations, she was beginning to see his advice in a new light. Maybe he wasn't criticizing her; maybe he was challenging her to step out of her comfort zone.

Before she could respond, the room's atmosphere shifted; laughter and whispered comments floated in from the dining room. The other ranch hands had quietly entered the dining room and had been watching their interaction with interest. Dawn's cheeks flushed with embarrassment.

"Go take your seat, Mr. Armstrong." She waved him off and he walked steadily back into the dining room.

Martha entered and Dawn's gaze shifted from Jet to her, the change in focus a welcome relief from the intensity of their encounter.

"Martha, any ideas which spice would brighten the taste of these potatoes?"

"Sure. Dill or parsley or basil."

Dawn reached past those spices and picked another.

"No, dear, not cinnamon."

Dawn winked at Martha. She carried the large tureen of mashed potatoes out to the dining room and walked around the table scooping a heapful onto each plate. Jet was last and before she scooped his, she quickly sprinkled them with cinnamon.

"Prepare to be dazzled, Mr. Armstrong."

Later, as they all ate together, she couldn't shake the memory of his gaze, the way his words had kindled something new within her. He ate the potatoes with relish and gave her an appraising bob of his head several times. And if a person could chuckle with just the eyes, that was what he did.

The evening's conversation eventually turned to more serious matters; Martha addressed the looming challenge the ranch faced, meaning the court battle, but the ranch hands were more focused on a different battle: that of finding a woman agreeable to marry one of them.

Pete flexed his muscles and said, "I've got a leg up on all of you. My boyish charm is said to be one of the greatest mysteries of modern time."

Chris smirked. "Well, ladies do tend to like a guy with a little mystique."

"You mean 'mistake,' if you're talking about Pete," Jet said. "And as for having a 'leg up' on any one, well ..." he tapped his prosthetic.

Corey laughed. "Yeah, you win there, Jet. But I've got the real vibes going ... musically, that is. I'm working on a ballad that will make a buckle bunny swoon."

There was plenty of disagreement there and several of the guys mimicked Corey's singing. Dawn listened with a light heart.

"Hey," Sawyer said, "come on guys. We all know women cannot resist a real cowboy. All we have to do is ride into town on a white horse and—"

"You're confusing cowboy with a knight in shining armor. Get your fairy tales straight, dude."

"White horse? Ha! With all the mud we ride through, no way."

"Hey," Matt finally joined in, "I'm gonna win, er, get a girl first. I've got the dance moves. You've seen me doing the two-step at the Circle Bar, haven't you?"

Pete pointed at him and laughed. "I have. Real smooth dance moves, Matty, you should be on that TV show." He got out of his chair and did a mocking imitation of Matt's dancing." Everyone laughed.

"Hey, Dawn, who do you think has the best chance of snagging a bride before the clock runs out?" Sawyer asked.

Dawn looked at them one by one. The laughter had abruptly stopped and they looked at her with expressions that revealed their subconscious thoughts: hope, reticence, pride, humility.

"Guys," she bit her lip, "you're all amazing. You're rugged, manly men." Her gaze lingered a moment on Jet. "I'm no fortune teller, but I can see each of you finding the right woman someday and living happily ever after." She got out of her chair.

"You gotta admit we clean up nice," Corey stated.

Tangled in Fate's Reins

"You do," Dawn smiled. "Now let me get the dessert and you can keep arguing among yourselves."

Chapter 6

THE MORNING SUN painted the Montana landscape in shades of gold and amber as Dawn stood at the edge of the ranch, her gaze fixed on the grazing horses on this her first day off. The boys would be eating pizza tonight, but right now most of them were off herding cattle or branding or something. She couldn't keep track. Day shifts, night shifts, teams. But they always left Jet behind to muck the stalls or do other chores, probably because he was the last one hired. It didn't occur to her that maybe his injury kept him from riding.

The breeze carried the gentle sound of hoofbeats, a soothing rhythm that called out to her in a way she relished. There was a particular desire working its way to her consciousness.

Taking a deep breath, she made her way to the stables, her heart fluttering with excitement and nervousness. Her eyes landed on Jet, who was tending to one of the horses, his focus intent. He had his shirt off, a glistening of sweat emphasizing his very appealing physique. She cleared her throat, trying to steady her voice.

"Hey, Jet. Can I ask you something?"

He turned to her, an element of surprise in his eyes. "Sure, what's on your mind?" He backed away from the horse, but caught the heel of his left boot on something and stumbled. He chuffed an embarrassed laugh, grabbed the shirt that was draped over the rail, and gave her a nice view of his rather awesome six-pack as he donned the shirt.

Dawn shifted her weight from one foot to the other, feeling a sudden shyness take hold of her. His muscular arms, broad shoulders, fine chest ... *umm.* She blinked hard to get her thoughts in line. The man was frowning. She'd forgotten he was an amputee. She probably startled him. Which leg was the prosthetic on? She couldn't tell. She forced her mouth to work, "I was wondering if you could teach me how to ride a horse."

Jet's eyebrows lifted in genuine surprise. "Ride a horse? Are you sure?"

She nodded, determination in her gaze. "Yeah, I think it's time I faced some of my fears. And I figured, who better to teach me than someone who loves horses?"

A soft smile tugged at the corners of Jet's lips. "Well, I'd be happy to help you, but are you sure you're up for it?" He finished buttoning the last button.

Dawn offered him a confident smile, her heart racing with anticipation but also anxiety. "Absolutely. So, when can we start?"

Jet introduced her to a gentle chestnut mare.

"She's a good horse?" Dawn wondered aloud.

"Yup, smarter than a cow. Her name is Bella ... but you can call her Cinnamon." He snickered.

She giggled. "Sorry about ruining your mashed potatoes the other night. I couldn't resist adding that dazzle."

"No problem. I'll eat anything you cook."

Dawn watched in awe as he expertly saddled the horse, his movements confident and assured, his balance as steady as a rock.

With a reassuring smile, Jet turned to her. He explained how to mount and held the horse as she did it. He handed her the reins but kept hold of the bridle. "Now, before we start, let's go over some basics."

Dawn bobbed her head, trying to absorb his instructions. But her nervousness began to bubble to the surface, causing her to fumble with the reins. Jet's calm patience was both encouraging and intimidating. Was it possible to be both frustrated and eager at the same time? She admired his ease with the horse and every time she looked down at him, she imagined him with the shirt off and wondered how nice it would be to lay her cheek against that warm shoulder.

He led them outside and explained the basics again.

In the corral, he had her circling him as he stood in the center and called out commands and encouragement. She got the hang of reining the horse, found it easy to sit the saddle at a trot, and once or twice relaxed her death grip on the pommel.

"Now you're ready to canter." Jet adjusted his Stetson and grinned. "Give her a nice squeeze with your heels and say, 'Canter.'"

"Wait, wait." Dawn pulled on the reins and stopped the mare. "I just want to go out and ride the trails, see nature, and not think about peeling potatoes or carrots. I don't need to learn how to run."

"Ah, but you need to know how to stick your ... uh ... the seat of your pants ... in the saddle and not fall off if the horse gets spooked and runs off."

"What could possibly spook Cinnamon? I mean Bella."

"A car, a dog, a snake, a gunshot, a bee, a wasp, a bird, a—"

"Okay, I get it. What do I do again?"

As they continued with her lesson, tension left the air; their conversation alternated between witty repartee and the necessary teaching instructions. Dawn felt a growing attraction toward Jet and not just because he was what her sister would call hot: handsome face, nice body. The guy was genuinely likable. She was determined to prove herself, yet his presence had an uncanny ability to throw her off balance.

Tangled in Fate's Reins

"You know, riding a horse is like dancing." Jet said. "It's all about finding the rhythm and trusting the steps."

"Do you dance?" She knew all about missed steps and awkward moves. She was afraid she'd just made one with that question.

His face darkened and he lifted his left leg and hopped on his right. "That's about it for me. I've had to strike certain activities off my list since—" he looked up at her "—you do know about my ... situation ... don't you?"

Dawn's cheeks flushed and she swallowed hard. She'd put her foot in her mouth for sure. "I heard something. You were in the military?"

"Right. A subject for another time. Here, give me the reins. I'll lead you on a tour of the section of land we might lose and you won't have to worry about the horse getting spooked with me holding the reins."

He opened the corral gate and led them through. She felt a bit guilty that she was riding and he was walking, but he didn't seem to be limping. She relaxed.

Their conversation drifted into a more personal realm, sharing snippets of their pasts as they went along summer paths.

Dawn hesitated for a moment, her natural inquisitiveness getting the best of her. "You know, I've noticed something," she began, watching him closely. "You seem to love the horses. You care for them and clean their stalls ... and I've seen the other guys riding, but never you. And you're not riding now. Is there a reason for that? I mean, I know there are riders in the Paralympics ..."

Jet's gaze turned distant, his fingers absently tracing the edges of Bella's bridle. "There's a story there, one that involves more than just horses."

Dawn's interest deepened, wondering if Jet carried another pain beneath his rugged exterior, something more than the amputation. "I'm listening." She sensed his vulnerability and hesitation.

He sighed, his gaze meeting hers for an instant. "I used to ride. I grew up with horses, and it was a big part of who I was. Would have competed in rodeos if my mother had allowed it." He snorted a laugh. "Funny. She was afraid I'd break my leg." He let out a long breath. "Then I went overseas and ... I lost my leg."

Dawn's heart tightened as she absorbed his words. "I'm so sorry."

Jet shrugged, his gaze drifting back to the horse. "It's been a struggle. Physically and emotionally. I'm afraid that if I try to ride again, I'll lose my balance, that I won't be able to hold on. I guess ... it's just silly pride."

Dawn would have liked to reach out and put her hand on his arm, but she was up high and he was walking in front of the horse now. "You know, I think you underestimate yourself."

He stepped to the side and glanced up at her, his eyes gleaming. "Maybe."

He stopped as they reached a look-out pinnacle. He tied the horse to a tree and held his hands out to help her dismount. He kept his hand against her back as they walked to the edge and looked across the land.

As they stood together, Dawn sensed an unspoken understanding bridging the gap between them. She wanted to open up in return and share a glimpse of her own past.

"I was orphaned just before I graduated high school. Car accident, lost both my parents," she confessed. "I was left to raise my younger sister, attend college online, all while trying to make ends meet with an inheritance that didn't last a year. I took out a ton of loans. I'm up to my eyebrows in debt, but my little sister's going to be a doctor in two more years ... if I can find, I mean, earn, the money to keep her in school."

Jet's gaze held hers, empathy shining in his eyes. "That's a heavy burden to carry."

Dawn nodded, her heart split with sadness and regret. "But I've never let it define me. And I don't think you should let your fears or your … disability … define you either."

A gentle smile tugged at Jet's lips, his gaze lingering on hers. "You're something else, Dawn."

Chapter 7

INSIDE THE RANCH'S bunkhouse, the atmosphere was a medley of grumblings and friendly teasing. The well-worn furniture creaked as Chris and Pete, two of the oldest ranch hands at twenty-eight and twenty-nine, lounged in the living room, their boots propped up on the coffee table. Laughter echoed against the walls as they debated animatedly.

"So, I'm telling you, Pete, I'm the more marriageable one here," Chris declared, a smug grin on his face.

Pete rolled his eyes, taking a playful sip from his beer. "Please, Chris. If anyone's marriage material, it's definitely me."

Chris leaned back, his arms crossed behind his head. "Oh, come on. I've got the charm, the charisma, and let's not forget my winning smile."

Pete scoffed. "Winning smile? More like a smirk only a mother could love."

Their banter continued as they good-naturedly argued over who was more likely to get a woman to marry him within six months. The mysterious benefactor's strange condition had been the source of much speculation among the ranch hands, and Chris and Pete's playful competition was proof of the challenge's intrigue.

As the debate reached a crescendo, the bunkhouse door creaked open, and Jet stepped inside. He leaned against the door frame, his expression unreadable. The room fell silent as all eyes turned toward him.

"Am I interrupting something?" Jet asked, his lips curling into a half-smile.

Chris and Pete exchanged glances before bursting into laughter. "Oh, Jet, perfect timing as always," Chris said, his tone lighthearted.

Pete bumped Jet playfully as he walked by. "Hey, settle something for us. Who do you think has a better shot at getting hitched in six months?"

Jet chuckled, taking a seat on one of the worn-out couches. "Well, it's hard to say. You both have your charms … if you can call burping and butt-scratching charming."

The razzing continued, the room filling with a lively energy that contrasted with the storm brewing outside. Boots lay scattered by the door, and a hole in the drywall from a past disagreement spoke of one of the many memories etched into the bunkhouse's walls.

As the conversation shifted to the looming court battle and the anonymous benefactor's offer, the light-heartedness gave way to a more serious tone.

Chris leaned forward, his expression more earnest. "You know, I'll bet the benefactor's money being tied to one of us getting married within six months is just a ploy to get out of paying up."

"But he's anonymous. That doesn't make sense." Jet rubbed his thigh and ignored the phantom pain that had worked its way up the non-existent leg.

Pete nodded in agreement. "Yeah, anonymous donors stay anonymous. But still, I wonder, just who is this guy? Why does he care about our love lives?"

Jet's gaze grew thoughtful, his downcast eyes distant for a moment. "It's strange, I agree. But if there's a chance to save the ranch, we should take it seriously." It was all he could do not to confess the part he played and the silly provision he'd thought up as a joke. He was going to be in big trouble when they found out.

Chris's voice held a note of skepticism. "What if he backs out, though? We can't rely on someone who's staying anonymous."

Pete eased into a more relaxed position, sighing. "Maybe we should think about a backup plan, just in case."

The room grew quiet, uncertainty settling over them like a storm cloud. And, as if to mirror their emotions, thunder rumbled outside, and rain began to pelt against the windows.

Jet broke the silence, his voice resolute. "You know what, guys? I think I know what would make a good backup plan. Plan B. How about a challenge of our own?"

Chris raised an eyebrow. "What kind of challenge?"

Jet's eyes sparkled with a mischievous glint. "A rodeo. We'll hold our own rodeo here at the ranch. It'll attract people, raise funds, and show the benefactor we're serious about our fight."

Pete chuckled, a grin spreading across his face. "A rodeo, huh? That could actually work. And you could be the announcer since you don't, uh, you don't ride anymore."

"Oh, I don't know about that. I climbed up on Martha's horse this morning ... just to get the feel of it again. The horse didn't mind that I had to mount from the wrong side. I might ..." he saw the looks on their faces and hesitated. These guys had seen him hopping around one-legged, coming out of the shower at night. They pitied him. They didn't think he'd ever ride again. Suddenly he lost his courage. "Well, scratch that. I'll be the announcer. Sounds good."

Chapter 8

THE RANCH SEEMED to hold its breath as the storm drew closer. Dark clouds loomed overhead, casting an eerie shadow over the land. Inside the ranch house, Dawn and Martha watched from the window, their faces pinched with concern. Old Duke padded from one to the other, allowing ear scratching and fur petting to help calm them.

The wind howled, whipping through the trees and rattling the windows. Martha clasped her hands together, her brow wrinkled with worry. "I hope the cattle are okay out there."

Dawn stretched her neck, her gaze fixed on the tumultuous sky. "Yeah, I can't imagine what the prairie must be like in this weather. There's nowhere to hide."

The storm raged on, lightning splitting the sky and thunder rumbling like a freight train. The walls of the ranch house seemed to shudder in response to nature's fury. Martha patted Duke extra hard, her voice tinged with unease. "Let's hope the boys can keep the cattle safe."

Out on the prairie, the ranch hands battled against the elements in a relentless effort to round up the frightened cattle. Pete, Chris, Matt, and three others worked together, their shouts barely audible over the howling wind.

Pete's voice was laced with urgency as he called out to the others. "We can't afford to lose any of them! Stay together and keep 'em moving!"

Rain drenched their clothes, and mud caked their horses' hooves as they pushed forward. The cattle were spooked, their eyes wide with fear as lightning flashed and thunder boomed. The ranch hands worked with quiet grit, each one knowing the importance of their task.

Jet was not content to be left behind. His heart raced as he led a horse out of the stable, the rain plastering his shirt to his skin. The storm had intensified, the lightning casting ghostly shadows on the ground. Despite the chaos of the weather, he was determined to try riding, to face his own fears head-on.

He had to mount from the wrong side, putting the only foot he had into the stirrup. He swung himself onto the saddle, throwing his prosthetic leg over, his grip tight on the pommel. The horse shifted uneasily, sensing his tension. Jet took a deep breath and tried to calm the animal. "Easy, girl. We've got this." He couldn't get the toe of his boot in the other stirrup, but he'd ridden bareback many times when he was younger and figured it wouldn't matter.

As he urged the horse forward, a bolt of lightning illuminated the landscape, revealing the panicked cattle in the distance. The horse beneath him snorted, its muscles tense. Jet's heart pounded in his chest as he tried to maintain control, but the horse's fear was contagious.

Another crack of lightning split the sky, and the horse reared up, its hooves kicking at the air. Jet's grip slipped, and before he could react, he was tumbling from the saddle. He hit the ground hard, the impact jarring his body. The horse bolted and galloped away into the storm.

Gritting his teeth against the pain, Jet pushed himself up onto his hands and knees, his prosthetic leg sinking into the mud. Rain noisily plinked off his rain poncho, and the world spun around him. Limping and crawling, he made his way back to the bunkhouse, his willpower unwavering.

When Pete and Matt returned to the bunkhouse, they found Jet on one of the couches, his wet hair plastered to his forehead. They exchanged glances.

Pete's voice held a note of worry as he looked at Jet. "You all right, Jet?"

He offered a faint smile, his voice full of exhaustion. "I'll be fine. Just took a bit of a tumble."

Chris glanced at Jet's mud-covered prosthetic leg. "Looks like you had quite an adventure out there."

Jet nodded, his gaze distant as he recounted his brief attempt at riding. "Yeah, didn't quite go as planned. Horse got spooked by the lightning or I could've been out there helping y'all."

Corey came in then and Chris sent him right back out to find the missing horse.

Pete clapped Jet on the shoulder. "You're a brave one, trying to ride for the first time in this weather."

Jet's lips quirked into a rueful grin. "Maybe not the best timing, but I had to give it a shot."

The storm outside continued to rage and Jet dipped his head at the others. "Hey, why don't a couple of you check on the ladies? Make sure everything's all right at the house."

Chapter 9

A DAY LATER the late afternoon sun cast warm hues across the walls of Dr. Langdon's office, the soft light creating a peaceful ambiance. The only reminders of last night's storm were puddles in the road. Jet sat in one of the comfortable chairs, his fingers idly tracing patterns on his jeans as he waited for the session to begin. He took a deep breath, reminding himself that opening up was part of the healing process.

Dr. Langdon, a seasoned psychologist with a gentle demeanor, settled into his chair across from Jet. "How have things been since we last met?"

Jet let himself settle back and focused on a point in the distance. "Busy, as always. Between the ranch, the court case, and everything else, it's been hectic."

Dr. Langdon waggled his head, his expression understanding. "Let's start with the court case. How's that been affecting you?"

Jet's shoulders tensed as he recounted the challenges of the impending court battle. "It's hard, you know? This place means so much to everyone here. And the idea of losing it, of letting it be bulldozed for a freeway ... it's a lot to process."

Dr. Langdon's voice held empathy. "Mm-hm."

Jet's gaze dropped to his hands, his fingers knotting together. "Yeah, and I feel like I've been trying to hold it all together, to make it work, even reaching out to my family."

Dr. Langdon's expression remained compassionate as he probed further. "And what was their response?"

Jet's jaw tightened, his voice tight with frustration. "They refused. Said it wasn't their problem. That I should focus on my 'real responsibilities.'"

Dr. Langdon jotted something in his notebook. "That must have been incredibly disappointing."

Jet's gaze flickered away, his fingers gripping the arms of the chair. "Yeah, it was. And it made me angry. That's why ... that's why I did what I did ... set up the anonymous benefactor monies from my trust. But ... I don't want to talk about that now."

The psychologist tilted forward slightly, his tone encouraging. "Jet, there's something else we could talk about. You mentioned attraction to someone new in your life. Would you be willing to explore that?"

Jet's cheeks flushed, his eyes flickering around the room. "Well, yeah, there's this new chef at the ranch. She's different, and I can't help but feel drawn to her."

"Attraction is a natural part of life. But do you think there's anything about this attraction that might be triggering for you?"

Jet's brow creased, his fingers tapping restlessly on his good knee. "Maybe ... I mean, I've been avoiding romantic relationships, focusing on work, ever since ..."

Langdon's voice was gentle as he finished Jet's sentence. "Since your return from combat."

Jet nodded, his gaze distant. "Yeah. I've had my fair share of nightmares and failures, and it feels like relationships are just another thing I could fail at."

Langdon reclined a bit, his tone encouraging. "It's important to remember that your worth isn't defined by success or failure in relationships. And it's okay to seek happiness, even if it feels daunting."

"I know. It's just ... hard to internalize sometimes."

Dr. Langdon wrote something else in his notebook, finished, and tapped his pen on the paper. "You know, Jet, it might help to share some of your thoughts and feelings with someone you trust. Maybe even the person you're attracted to."

Jet's eyebrows lifted in surprise. "You think so?" He ran his fingers along the stubble on his chin.

Dr. Langdon nodded. "Opening up about your fears and vulnerabilities can create a deeper connection."

Jet hesitated for a moment before reaching for the leather-bound notebook he'd brought with him. "I've been keeping a journal. Would it be helpful if I read some parts of it to her?"

"I think that could be a great idea. Why don't you practice on me."

Jet flipped open the journal, his voice steady as he read aloud:

"*June 12th: There are nights when the memories refuse to stay buried. The horror of it all hits me, and I'm back there, in the chaos and fear. I try to put on a brave face, but deep down, the past still haunts me.*"

Jet took a deep breath before continuing:

"July 3rd: Sometimes, I catch myself wanting to reach out, to break down the walls I've built. But then the fear of rejection hits me, and I retreat. It's like I'm stuck in this cycle of isolation."

Dr. Langdon angled toward his patient, his expression compassionate. "It sounds like you're aware of the patterns you've created. And awareness is the first step toward change."

Jet's fingers tightened around the journal, his voice quieter now:

"August 20th: The ranch is my refuge, my sanctuary. I've poured everything into it, hoping it will fill the void inside. But maybe it's time to let others in, to share the burden and find a way to heal."

As Jet closed the journal, he looked up at Dr. Langdon. "I want to heal, to move forward. But sometimes, it's just so discouraging."

"Healing takes time, Jet. And you're taking steps in the right direction. Remember, it's okay to ask for help and to let others in."

As Jet left Dr. Langdon's office, he thought about the advice to share his thoughts with the woman who'd captured his interest. Could he? Would he? Perhaps he'd start by cutting his jeans off at the knee. It was hard getting the prosthetic on and off with jeans or long pants, but he'd always thought it falsely proud for amputees to flaunt their mechanical limbs as if they were something to be proud of.

But maybe not. Maybe it was just more convenient and to heck with the pitying looks and phony sympathy. Maybe he wanted to see Dawn's reaction. Rip the Band-Aid off and see if he had a chance with her.

Chapter 10

THE GUYS WARNED her at noon that they might be late for supper, so Dawn kept everything warm on the stove until she heard the hoofbeats pounding past the ranch house. Twenty minutes later the men were washed up and ready to dive into the food as soon as Martha said grace.

The clinking of utensils against plates filled the air, mingling with laughter and the satisfying hum of conversation. Jet sat at the end of the table, his gaze occasionally drifting toward Dawn, who was engrossed in a conversation with Chris.

As the meal came to an end, Jet stood up, his chair scraping against the floor. All eyes turned toward him as he swept his hand down and across the cut-off ends of his jeans. A nicely muscled calf, visible between the jean's knee and the cowboy boot's top, didn't match the other leg. The prosthetic limb, ending in a well-worn cowboy boot, reflected the light off its metal trimmings. The room fell silent, the only sound the soft ticking of the grandfather clock in the next room.

Dawn's gaze flickered to Jet's leg before meeting his eyes. Her expression held acceptance and respect. Jet wanted to believe it was a silent acknowledgment of the courage it took for him to reveal this part of himself. Then he noticed the small smile tugging at the corner of her lips, and she raised her glass in a toast.

"To Jet and his service to our country."

"Here, here."

Jet's heart swelled at her gesture, his affection for her growing by leaps and bounds. He had feared that his prosthetic would be a barrier between them, but her approval shattered those fears like a fragile glass. He made his way to the kitchen to help with the cleaning up and made sure the door to the dining room was closed so his buddies wouldn't observe whatever awkward advances he tried.

"It's not your turn to help," Dawn said. "Did you lose a bet with Pete or something?"

"No ... I won," he said, tucking in the silver chain that held the dog tags he still kept against his chest.

Jet started rinsing dishes and loading the dishwasher, his gaze occasionally drifting to Dawn. "You know, you're quite the chef. I'm starting to look forward to meals here."

"Starting to?" Dawn chuckled as she filled two containers with leftovers. "Well, I aim to please. It's not every day you get a chance to cook for a ranch full of hungry cowboys."

Jet grinned, his eyes going bluer. "But it is every day for you. You've been amazing. These guys used to complain when the other cook, Brian, was putting flowers on our plates, and everything was some French word like *quiche*. Thank you for not making us cowboys eat frog legs or escargot."

"You're welcome." She gulped. "I used to help my mom in the kitchen before she ... well, of course, it was before ..."

Jet moved closer. "She must have taught you a lot because I think I've put on five pounds since you came here."

"Me, too. I sample everything, several times, as I'm cooking. Especially the desserts." She looked at him. "Have you ever wondered why there are not leftover desserts for the next day?" Her eyebrows rose and twitched. "I eat them."

Jet laughed with her.

As they finished tidying up, their conversation shifted to the topic that had been on everyone's minds—the anonymous benefactor's strange condition. Jet leaned against the counter, his voice hinting at amusement. "So, the benefactor wants a wedding to take place at the ranch. Have you or Martha considered getting in on that?"

Dawn rolled her eyes playfully. "As a matter of fact, I've had three proposals this week. But a ranch wedding? Nope, I'd never marry one of those cowboys."

Jet raised an eyebrow, his lips curling into a teasing smile. "Is that so? And what kind of man would you marry, then?"

Dawn's cheeks flushed, her eyes narrowing as she shot him a mock glare. "Nice try, Jet. I'm not falling for that one. I'll give a characteristic and you'll say that fits Pete … or Matt … or whoever, and then you'll say I'd be perfect for … whoever."

Jet chuckled, the playful raillery between them filling the room with warmth, both forgetting about his prosthetic. He gazed at Dawn, his expression growing thoughtful. "You know, it's interesting, trying to figure out what someone wants in a partner."

Dawn's gaze softened, her voice quieter now. "Oh, I know what I want. I want what my parents had."

"Tell me about them."

"Well," she took a seat at the small kitchen table and Jet grabbed the other chair. When he sat, his mechanical knee touched hers, but she didn't react. "Um, my dad was honest and funny and … always there. Until he wasn't." Her eyes got misty. "That's what I want, an honest man. Oh, and he has to be a Christian." She gave him a pointed look.

"And none of these men who proposed to you this week fits the bill?"

"No, they don't. And I wonder if any of you will manage to snag a gal who will get married just to save this ranch."

"Well, if *you* love this ranch and *you* won't marry a cowboy … then I don't suppose we have a chance of meeting the benefactor's condition."

"I didn't say I wouldn't marry a *cowboy*; I said I wouldn't marry any of *those* cowboys." She tilted her head toward the dining room.

Jet's throat tightened. "Hmm, well … I'm not one of *those* cowboys. What if we make a pact that if no one has fulfilled the silly requirement by, say, Christmas, then, uh, you and I …"

He didn't finish, but he didn't have to. Dawn was already nodding her head. "Sure, it's a deal."

Martha came in then with dessert plates they'd missed and Dawn jumped up to start the dishwasher.

Later, Jet retreated to his room with a sense of contentment. He picked up his leather-bound journal, its pages filled with his thoughts and reflections. As he sat on the edge of his bed, he began to write, his pen moving with purpose.

August 24th: Certain words linger in my mind—the idea that you find what you're looking for in unexpected places. Dawn is what and who I'm looking for. I want to be the kind of man she described. Someone who listens, supports, and stands by her side. I want to be the one she can count on, the one who makes her laugh and feel cherished. And who's always there for her. An honest man. I'll have to work on that because I haven't been totally honest with anyone here.

Chapter 11

THE MOON CAST a gentle glow over the ranch, illuminating the quiet beauty of the night. Dawn paced back and forth in her room, her thoughts in turmoil. She chastised herself for being so forward as to agree to marry Jet to save the ranch. It felt like a reckless decision, one driven by desperation or a flirty impulse rather than genuine feelings ... though she did feel something.

Her heart was a tangled mess of emotions, and she needed someone to talk to. With a determined exhale, she left her room and made her way to Martha's door, her knuckles rapping softly against the wood.

"Come in," Martha's voice called from inside.

Dawn entered to find Martha sitting in a cozy armchair, a book in her lap, the German Shepherd at her feet. The warm light from a lamp cast a soft glow, accentuating the lines on Martha's face. Martha looked up and smiled warmly. "Dawn, dear. What can I do for you?"

Dawn hesitated, her words catching in her throat for a moment. "I ... I need some advice, Martha."

Martha set her book aside, her gaze steady and inviting. "Of course, dear. Sit down. Let's talk."

Tangled in Fate's Reins

Dawn took a seat on the edge of a second chair, her fingers fidgeting with the hem of her shirt. "It's about Jet. I mean, I know it's crazy, but I think I just agreed to marry him to save the ranch ... if no one else does by Christmas. And now ... now I'm second-guessing myself. Half regretful, half super excited. I don't know if he took me seriously or ..."

Martha's expression softened, her eyes kind as she bent forward. "Dawn, marriage is a serious commitment. It's natural to have doubts, especially when it's not based on love."

Dawn bowed her head, her voice shaky. "I just don't want to hurt him. He's been through so much, and he deserves someone who truly loves him."

"You're right to consider his feelings. But let me share something with you, something I wish someone had told me when I was your age."

Dawn's gaze lifted, her curiosity piqued. "What?"

Martha's voice was gentle as she spoke, her eyes distant as if lost in a memory. "I married young, thinking it was the right thing to do because ... well, we had gone too far and with my Christian upbringing I felt guilty and thought the only thing to do was to get married. But I didn't truly love him and I finally realized he didn't care for me either. He had several affairs. It ended in divorce, and that's how I ended up with this ranch. Then I met Paul," her face brightened, "and we had an amazing life until he passed. He was the love of my life." Her eyes teared up and the tiny muscles at her mouth twitched.

Dawn's eyebrows tilted in surprise. "I knew you were widowed, but I didn't know you were married twice."

Martha nodded, her gaze returning to Dawn. "Yes, and I learned a valuable lesson from each experience. Love is the only foundation for a strong marriage. It's what makes the journey worthwhile, even in the face of challenges."

Dawn's gaze dropped, her thoughts spinning. "I don't want to end up in a marriage that lacks love. But I also don't want you to lose the ranch. I suppose we could go into the marriage expecting to get divorced once the lawsuit is over."

"One should never get married thinking divorce is an option." Martha reached out, placing a reassuring hand on Dawn's. "It's a difficult position to be in, my dear. But remember, love can't be forced or rushed. And it's okay to have doubts, especially when something as important as a marriage is at stake. I wish this benefactor hadn't made that silly condition."

Dawn looked up at Martha, her eyes searching. "What do you think I should do, Martha?"

Martha's gaze was steady. "Listen to your heart, Dawn. Take your time, and don't let anyone pressure you into making a decision to save the ranch. It won't kill me if I lose it."

Dawn sighed, her shoulders relaxing as the weight of her foolish promise lifted slightly. "Thank you, Martha. Your advice means a lot."

Martha smiled warmly, her eyes twinkling with kindness. "Of course, dear. Now, let me share something with you about Jet."

Dawn tilted her head, interested. "What is it?"

Martha's expression grew tender as she began to speak, her voice full of affection for Jet. "Jet is a remarkable man, Dawn. He's faced challenges that would break others, but he's persevered with a strength and fortitude that's truly inspiring. He's kind, caring, and has a heart of gold. Obviously, you know, because he's willing to marry a stranger, too, to save *my* ranch. There's really nothing in it for him ... except, I suppose," she laughed, "he'll have a job for life here and he'll have a wife. Personally, though, I think he's in love with you."

Dawn's gaze softened, her heart warmed by Martha's words. "He's been through so much, and yet he's still willing to help others, to fight for the ranch."

Martha nodded, a soft smile on her lips. "Exactly. Jet's character shines through in every action he takes. He's someone worth getting to know, someone who could bring happiness to your life."

Dawn wanted to hear more. "Do you know ... did he have a girlfriend before? Before he lost his leg?"

Martha looked down and then stared straight at Dawn. "I'm not supposed to know ... but Pete told me. He was engaged to be married, but she left him before he even got out of the hospital." Her lips went white as she pressed them tightly together in anger and disgust.

"That's horrible," Dawn stood up. Duke rose, too, and paced around her. "That woman didn't deserve him." She walked toward the door and then back. "Martha ... I'd like to stay on. I haven't had any luck in my job search. Truth be told, I haven't wanted to find anything. Do you think you could find something else for me to do when your cook returns?"

"Besides marrying Jet?" Martha laughed. "As a matter of fact, unless you can ride and rustle cattle, do some branding, help the vet with inoculations ... well, I don't think there's anything else you could do here."

Dawn sighed and gave Duke a petting.

Martha went on. "So, I guess you'll just have to stay on as chef," she lifted her phone off the table and wiggled it, "because I got a call today from my Brian who found a restaurant willing to pay him twice what I can afford."

"That's great … I mean, great for him, maybe not so great for you, but …"

"It's great for all of us. I much prefer having you here … and I'm sure so does Jet."

Chapter 12

THE FOLLOWING DAY Dawn heard a noisy car rev its engine as it pulled up to the ranch. There were several honks and then a pounding on the front door. Martha was in town, the boys on the range, and Jet in the barn. It was up to Dawn to see who was so insistently knocking. She hoped to heaven it wasn't anything to do with the lawsuit.

Her breath caught as she saw the back of a man in a suit. He had knocked again and had turned to leave. She opened the door and stepped out.

"Hello, what can I do for you? Martha, the ranch owner, isn't here right now."

The man turned and she nearly fell over. It was her former boss, Richard Stanton.

She stood on the porch of the ranch house, her hands dusted with smudges of flour from her baking. The day had been busy, and the scent of freshly baked bread still lingered in the air. Frozen in surprise, she stared at the man who had made her life miserable for too long, and a sense of great anxiety loomed over her.

Her contentment and peace of moments before were now shattered. Her heart sank as the tall, imposing figure leered at her, his expensive suit contrasting starkly with the rustic surroundings.

"Mr. Stanton," she barely got his name out, "what do you want?"

His voice dripped with condescension as he addressed her. "Dawn Dupree, I should have known I'd find you in some sorry, dirty place like this. But find you I did."

Dawn's jaw tightened, her fingers curling into fists at her sides. She straightened her spine, summoning the strength to ask again. "Mr. Stanton. What are you doing here?"

Stanton's gaze flickered to the ranch around him, a sneer playing at the corners of his lips. "I came to collect what's owed to my company. You left quite a mess behind, didn't you?"

Dawn's voice held a measure of defiance. "You fired me on the spot. I didn't have a chance to clean out my desk. But just so you know, if you hadn't fired me, I would have left eventually anyway. The environment there was toxic and it was your fault."

Stanton's face reddened, his temper flaring. "Toxic environment? You think you can just waltz away from the damage you've caused? The broken computer, missing laptops, printers, and money stolen from my desk!"

Dawn's eyes blazed with anger. "I didn't take anything! And you know it."

Stanton's demeanor shifted from anger to something darker, his voice dripping with venom. "You always were a troublemaker, a good-for-nothing." His voice got so loud Dawn was sure the cowboys on the prairie would hear him.

She shouted back just as loudly and stood her ground.

Tangled in Fate's Reins

The tension escalated. Out of the corner of her eye Dawn saw a movement at the stable. Clutching a pitchfork in his hand, Jet strode toward the porch, his gaze locking onto Stanton's threatening presence.

"Dawn, everything all right?" Jet called, still yards away. His voice was firm, his eyes narrowing as he assessed the situation.

Dawn's shoulders relaxed, her anxiety easing as Jet approached. "Jet, this is Richard Stanton, my former boss."

Jet's voice held a warning edge as he addressed Stanton. "Is there a problem?"

Stanton's eyes widened slightly as he took in Jet's imposing figure and the pitchfork in his hand. He sneered, his bravado not fully masking his discomfort. "No problem here. Just discussing a little business matter."

Jet's eyes bore into Stanton's, his voice unwavering. "I suggest you leave, Mr. Stanton."

Stanton's bravado faltered as he took a step back, his face reddening further. "Fine, I'll go. But mark my words, Dawn, if I don't have $5000 by the end of the week, I'll be involving the police."

With that, Stanton turned on his heel and retreated to his car, the engine roaring to life as he sped away from the ranch.

Dawn let out a shaky breath, her hands trembling slightly. Jet tossed the pitchfork away and stepped closer to her, his presence a comforting anchor. She buried her face in his shoulder, tears welling up in her eyes as the awfulness of the encounter washed over her.

"What was that all about?" he asked.

She gave him a quick summary. "I didn't steal anything, Jet. I swear."

His arms encircled her, his voice soft and reassuring. "I believe you, Dawn. You don't have to prove anything to anyone."

Her breath hitched as she clung to him, her emotions spilling over. "It's just ... it's not fair. He fired me so suddenly I didn't even gather my personal items. I didn't take anything and I don't know how I prove I'm innocent."

As Dawn leaned against Jet, something shifted. The shared moment created an intimacy that she couldn't ignore. Her heart raced as he looked down at her, his gaze drawn to her lips, a magnetic pull urging her to close the distance between them.

In a moment of suspended time, their lips hovered inches apart, the air charged with new emotion. But just as their connection was about to deepen, Jet took a wobbly step back, the heel of his boot catching the lip of the first step off the porch. His balance wavered, she tried to help, and they tumbled off the porch together, landing in a heap on the grass.

"Oh, I'm so, so sorry."

"It's all right," Jet rolled aside. "I'm just glad we didn't land on that thing."

Dawn stared at the farm implement. "I wish you had stuck him with it."

"Right," he twisted so he could get himself up without assistance, "and then we'd have another lawsuit to contend with."

Dawn rose, too, and brushed some debris off her jeans. She noticed Jet wincing as he got upright.

"You know what?" she said with a laugh. "You were like a chivalrous knight, coming to my aid. I haven't properly thanked you." Without another moment's hesitation, she put both hands on his shoulders and tilted her face up.

The kiss was sweet and thrilling. But it didn't last more than a second.

"Well," Jet said, their heads still only inches apart, "you're welcome. And … now let *me* thank *you.*"

His arms enfolded her. She slipped her hands further around his back. She was vaguely aware that his kiss was much more insistent. His chest heaved against hers and she opened her eyes for a moment to see his lashes against his tightly closed lids. Her own eyes fluttered shut and she enjoyed every sensation that filled her. This man knew how to kiss a woman. She had no breath but his, no heartbeat but his, no thought but his. She was lost in his kiss; she sank into his arms, his face, his hands.

"I … I …" she stuttered when he finally released her, "uh, what are you thanking *me* for?"

Jet turned and picked up the pitchfork. "You'll figure it out," he said as he walked back to the barn.

Chapter 13

THE SUN CAST a fall-is-coming glow over the ranch as Martha's pickup truck rumbled down the gravel road. Jet sat in the passenger seat, his gaze drifting over the sweeping expanse of the prairie. Martha had offered to drive him into town since she had a meeting with lawyers, and he had some errands to run.

Martha glanced at Jet, her face. "You seem a bit lost in thought, young man."

Jet's lips curled into a small grin. "Just thinking about things, Martha."

Martha's laugh was warm and hearty. "Ah, the joys of thinking. I've been doing a bit of that myself."

They shared a comfortable silence as the town came into view, the architecture of the buildings reflecting the history of the place. Martha pulled up in front of the bank, bringing the truck to a smooth stop.

"I'll be meeting with the lawyers. You go ahead and run your errands, and I'll pick you up when I'm done."

Jet nodded, easing out of the truck, his good leg first, then his prosthetic, clearly visible since he had dared to wear the cut-off jeans. "Sounds like a plan. Thanks, Martha."

As the truck drove away, Jet walked into the bank, the familiar smell of paper and polished wood filling his nostrils. The hushed tones of conversation and the creaking of old floorboards underfoot lent an air of times past to the place. He noticed one of the tellers, Ashley her nameplate said, and remembered her as a teen barrel racer. That made him think perhaps the rodeo they were planning should include some female events.

He gave the young woman a quick nod and then approached another counter, where the bank manager, Mr. Thompson, greeted him with a warm smile. "Good morning, Mr. Armstrong. How can I assist you today?"

Jet returned the smile, his expression friendly yet determined. "I need to arrange a payment to Richard Stanton."

Mr. Thompson's eyebrows lifted in surprise. "Ah, I see. We can certainly help you with that. Let's go into my office."

As Jet and Mr. Thompson discussed the transaction, their conversation shifted to a more personal tone. Jet bowed forward slightly, his voice earnest. "Mr. Thompson, I've been meaning to talk to you about something else."

"Of course, Mr. Armstrong. What's on your mind?"

Jet hesitated for a moment before continuing. "It's about the ranch, about the court case. I know there's an anonymous benefactor who's helping with the funds for the fight against the freeway."

Mr. Thompson's expression remained attentive. "Yes, that's correct. The identity of the benefactor remains confidential."

Jet's gaze held steady, his voice firm. "Mr. Thompson, I am the anonymous benefactor. I arranged it through my lawyer." He set a small white business card with his lawyer's name on it in front of the bank manager.

Mr. Thompson's eyes widened slightly, surprise and realization dawning in his gaze. "You?"

Jet nodded, a sense of quiet resolve in his demeanor. He pulled back the card. "Yes, and I've been quietly helping Martha with the mortgage payments and other expenses for a while now."

Mr. Thompson regarded Jet with respect. "Your generosity has made a significant difference, Mr. Armstrong."

Jet's fingers tapped lightly on the edge of the desk, his expression conflicted. "I've been debating whether or not to reveal my identity. Part of me thinks it's time to let everyone know. But another part of me worries about the impact it might have on the ranch and the people involved."

Mr. Thompson frowned, his voice thoughtful. "It's a delicate balance, Mr. Armstrong. Revealing your identity could change things, but it could also inspire others to contribute. Ultimately, the decision is yours and I'll abide by it."

Jet's gaze shifted to the marble columns in the bank, the indecision evident in his eyes. "I'll have to think about it. But for now, I'd like to arrange the payment to Stanton without revealing my involvement."

Mr. Thompson dipped his head, his expression understanding. "Certainly, Mr. Armstrong. We'll proceed as requested."

Tangled in Fate's Reins

As Jet left the bank, his mind was a swirl of thoughts and emotions. His heart felt lighter. He had made his decision, one that aligned with his growing feelings toward Dawn.

Chapter 14

IT WAS ANOTHER gorgeous Montana morning, the air alive with the sound of hooves and the energetic banter of the ranch hands. Pete, Chris, Matt, and the others mounted their horses, ready for a day of riding herd. One of them brought up the plans for the upcoming rodeo.

Pete rode out first, his head turned back to the others, his voice loud with bravado. "You know, I once rode the meanest bronc this side of the river. Sent me flying headfirst into the dirt, but I managed to hold on for a solid eight seconds."

Chris smirked and urged his horse forward. "Yeah, and at that same rodeo I roped a calf in record time. Still got the trophy to prove it."

Chase joined in with a confident grin. "You guys might be good, but I'm telling you, I can beat any cowboy from the surrounding ranches in steer wrestling."

Matt chuckled, his head nodding back to where Jet was entering the stable, well out of earshot. "Well, I remember seeing Jet compete in junior events before his family moved east. He had some awesome skills … back then."

Tangled in Fate's Reins

The mention of Jet's past stirred a ripple of comments among the group. One ranch hand unnecessarily lowered his voice. "Hey, speaking of Jet, I heard a rumor that his family's got money. Like, rich beyond belief."

A round of skeptical laughter erupted among the men, disbelief on their faces. "Come on, guys," Pete chimed in. "You really think someone with a fat bank account would enlist in the military and take those kinds of risks? And then spend his life mucking out stalls? No way."

The discussion continued off and on throughout the day as the ranch hands herded cattle, their voices rising above the rhythmic clopping of hooves. Of course, other topics came up as well, two favorites being sports and women.

As they returned to the ranch late that afternoon, they encountered Jet in the barn, engrossed in his work.

Pete approached Jet with a smirk, his tone daring. "Hey, Jet, we were just having a little debate about your family's fortune. Millionaires or billionaires?"

Jet looked up, his expression a mix of annoyance and mild exasperation. "Hah. Definitely not billionaires, but ... I don't really know. I'm not in the loop."

Chris frowned. "Some of the guys here seem to think you're rolling in dough."

Jet's lips twitched into a half-smile, his tone casual. "Dough? Is that what you call this muck?"

Pete finished unsaddling and said, "Seriously, guys, lay off him. He's not going to hand out hundred-dollar bills any time soon."

"Wish I could," Jet said. "I understand your 'thirst for knowledge.' Let me put it this way. My father started a company that quickly took off ..."

The ranch hands exchanged knowing looks, their teasing grins intensifying. "Ah, we knew it! So, you're secretly a trust-fund kid, after all?"

Jet's laughter sounded forced as he shook his head. "Not quite. I traded my inheritance for a life here on the ranch. Turns out, money doesn't mean much when you're seeking something more fulfilling."

Pete slapped Jet on the back, his grin broadening. "Well, whatever the story, we're glad to have you here, Jet. Fortune or not, it's still your turn to buy the beer."

Tangled in Fate's Reins

Chapter 15

THE DAY'S WORK had come to an end, and the ranch was wrapped in the soft hues of twilight. Jet stood near the stable, his gaze fixed on the silhouette of Chris who was taking extra time grooming his horse. Taking a deep breath, Jet walked over, his expression determined.

"Hey, Chris. Can I talk to you for a minute?"

Chris turned, an easy smile forming as he answered. "Of course, buddy. What's on your mind? And, hey, don't worry about those guys trying to figure out your financial status." He patted his horse.

Jet hesitated for a moment, his gaze dropping to the ground before he met Chris's eyes. "Yeah, I don't mind all that, but what I do mind is watching you all ride out and not being able to join you." His sigh was audible. "I want to start riding again, but I need some help figuring out the best way to mount, dismount, all the rest. I was wondering if you could help me."

Chris's expression softened, his eyes filled with understanding. "Absolutely, Jet. I'd be happy to help. I know I'd miss it, too, if I couldn't ride. So … with your prosthetic, uh, … "

Thankfulness and determination filled Jet's voice. "That's the problem. I know it won't be easy, but I want to try. I want to overcome this."

Chris clapped Jet on the shoulder, his support unwavering. "I admire your spirit. Especially after that tumble you took in the storm. We can practice in the evenings after supper ... provided there isn't lightning. Sound good?"

"Yeah, thanks."

For the next few nights, after supper had been cleared away, and the others occupied themselves with a poker game or an odd chore for Martha, Chris and Jet ventured to the riding arena. Under the canopy of stars, with the moon as their silent witness, Chris guided Jet through the process of mounting a horse and adjusting his posture to accommodate his prosthetic leg. It was a slow and often frustrating process, but Jet's resolve remained steadfast.

As they took breaks between attempts, Chris leaned against the fence, his voice casual as he tried to distract Jet from his growing frustration and the obvious pain. "So, any of the guys found a woman to marry yet? You know, to save the ranch?"

Jet's eyebrows lifted, his gaze flickering to Chris. "You think any of them would actually go through with it?"

Chris shrugged, a playful smile on his lips. "Hard to say. I've been texting a woman who seems great, but I've yet to meet her in person. Corey's the one most likely to find someone, though. He's got that charming smile and all, plays the guitar, sings pretty good."

Jet's grip on the top fence rail tightened, his chest tightening with a fear he couldn't quite identify. "And what about the rest of the guys?"

Chris's eyes lit up with mischief as he glanced at Jet. "Well, let's just say, there's some friendly competition. But I've noticed quite a few eyes on a certain chef."

Jet's heart clenched at the mention of Dawn, a surge of emotion coursing through him. He tried to play it cool, his voice nonchalant. "Dawn? Really?"

Chris chuckled, a knowing look in his eyes. "Yeah, she's got that whole helpless little blonde thing going for her. Plus, she's easy on the eyes."

Jet's jaw tensed, his fingers curling into fists. He struggled to keep his emotions in check; the idea of other guys pursuing Dawn stirred something fierce within him. "Is that so?"

Chris's gaze turned sympathetic as he met Jet's eyes. "Hey, Jet, you okay?"

Jet forced a smile, his tone strained. "Yeah, just tired from the riding practice, I guess."

Chris's expression softened, his voice gentle. "Look, if you ever need someone to talk to, you know I'm here, right?"

Jet nodded. "Thanks, Chris."

As they resumed their practice, the moonlight casting long shadows on the ground, Jet's thoughts were a whirlwind of emotions. He grappled with jealousy, anger, and a yearning he couldn't deny. As he faced the challenges of riding with a prosthetic leg, he also confronted the turmoil of his own heart, the emotions that Dawn had awakened within him. He very nearly told Chris of the impulsive pact he'd made with Dawn, then thought better of it.

Chapter 16

THE SUNDAY MORNING sun painted the world in hues of pink and gold as Martha's pickup truck rolled along the dusty road, carrying Martha and Dawn to their quaint little church. Martha's hands gripped the steering wheel with practiced ease, a serene smile gracing her lips. Beside her, Dawn glanced out the window, lost in thought.

As the truck bumped along the road, Dawn finally broke the silence. "Martha, can I ask you something?"

Martha blinked repeatedly as she glanced at Dawn. "Of course, dear."

Dawn's voice was hesitant as she voiced her thoughts. "I've been wondering … why don't any of the ranch hands come to church with us?"

Martha's lips curved into a thoughtful smile. "Oh, sometimes they do. Off and on. Mostly off. I've been working on that, dropping hints here and there, and, of course, praying. But you know, faith is a personal journey, and it's up to each of them to find his way to God … or back to God."

Dawn knitted her brows, a trace of uncertainty in her face. "I guess I understand that, but it makes me wonder. I've been thinking a lot about my own path lately."

"What's been on your mind, dear?"

Dawn's fingers played with the material of her dress, her voice soft. "Well ... faith is important to me. My father was a devout Christian, and he always told my sister and me to seek out men of faith, men who would honor and respect us, and who would put God first."

Martha's brow contracted slightly. "Dawn, is there something you're not telling me?"

Dawn's sigh held a breath of conflict. "It's just that ... I have these doubts, Martha. About ... Jet. He's an amazing man, and I care about him so much and think about him all the time ... but I don't know if he's a Christian."

Martha's hand reached out to gently touch Dawn's arm, her voice filled with compassion. "I heard him praying once ... on the porch. I think he believes in God, but he's angry still. Angry about losing his leg and probably about losing his fiancée. Maybe you should ask him to join us next Sunday."

Dawn tapped a finger on the Bible in her lap. "Okay, maybe I will."

"Dawn, the path of love is not always clear, and sometimes our hearts are in turmoil. It's okay to have doubts and questions. What's important is to be true to yourself and to listen to your heart. That seems to be where you can best hear God's voice."

Dawn's gaze met Martha's, confusion and indecision warring in her eyes. "I know you're right, Martha. It's just ... there's so much going on: the ranch, the lawsuit, my old boss threatening me, the marriage pact ..."

Martha's smile was gentle and reassuring. "Life has a way of presenting us with challenges, dear. But it's in facing those challenges that we grow and discover who we truly are." She chuckled brightly. "And … everything always works out. You'll see."

Inside the quaint church, the congregation sat in the wooden pews, washed in the soft glow of sunlight filtering through stained glass windows. Pastor Mike stood at the pulpit, his voice carrying a sense of serenity as he spoke.

"Dear friends, in this journey of life, we often find ourselves at crossroads, faced with choices that shape our paths. It's natural to question and wonder, to doubt and to seek guidance. But in the dark well of doubt, there is one constant: God has a plan for each one of us."

Dawn's eyes were fixed on the pastor, his words resonating with her own struggles. Pastor Mike continued, his gaze warm and comforting.

"Trusting in God's plan doesn't mean that our paths will be smooth or free of challenges. It means that we have faith that, even in the midst of the unknown, God is guiding us toward a purpose greater than our own understanding."

As the sermon continued, Dawn's heart began to feel lighter. She listened to the pastor's words, finding solace in the idea that her doubts and uncertainties were part of a greater tapestry, woven by a loving and guiding hand. And, she realized, she desperately hoped that within that pattern more than one thread led to Jet.

Chapter 17

WHILE THE LADIES sat in church, the ranch hands gathered around the long wooden table for their Sunday morning breakfast of cold cereal. Laughter and chatter filled the air as bowls clattered, cereal spilled, and coffee mugs were filled to the brim. Corey grinned, his face slightly flushed as he announced last night's date ended with a promise for another next Saturday.

Sawyer, the perpetual jokester, nudged Corey playfully. "Well, well, looks like someone's got himself a new flame. Tell us more. How'd it go?"

Corey rolled his eyes, a grin tugging at his lips. "It went fine, Sawyer. Just fine."

Chase joined in with a wink. "Just fine? I bet it was more than fine, judging by that grin."

Laughter erupted, and the table was alive with ribbing and teasing. Jet's gaze swept across the rowdy scene, a twinkle of amusement in his eyes. "All right, all right, settle down, you bunch of hooligans."

The noise level gradually lowered as the ranch hands looked at Jet expectantly, most of them shoveling spoonfuls of various cereals into their mouths. Jet cleared his throat, his expression serious. "I want to talk about the upcoming rodeo. It's only a few weeks away, and there's a lot to prepare."

He leaned forward, his voice carrying authority. "Sawyer, I need you to handle contacting the stock contractors for the bulls and bucking broncs. Pete, you're in charge of getting in touch with the radio station for advertising. Chase, you'll handle setting up the ticket sales and promotions. And Corey, I need you to oversee the setup and management of the rodeo grounds. That shouldn't conflict with those evenings I know you're off singing at that bar."

"Whoa," Sawyer said, "sounds like you've spent a lot of time thinking up everything."

Jet turned to Matt. "Matt, you've got concessions covered, right?"

"You bet, boss. We'll have the best darn food truck rodeo grub in the county."

Jet's gaze settled on Chris and he cleared his throat. "Chris, I want you to help me secure sponsors and donors. We need all the support we can get to make this rodeo a success."

The atmosphere grew more serious as Jet's words hung in the air. Corey's brow furrowed, concern in his eyes. "Jet, what if the anonymous benefactor backs out? We need that money for the lawsuit. We can't be sure we'll make enough from the rodeo to cover the lawsuit."

A tense silence followed Corey's question. Jet hesitated for a moment, his gaze shifting to the table. "I can assure you that the benefactor won't back out. There's a plan in place."

Tangled in Fate's Reins

With their curiosity aroused, the ranch hands exchanged puzzled glances. Sawyer leaned in, raising a wet spoon in Jet's direction, a mischievous smile on his face. "All right, Jet, spill the beans. What's the plan?"

Jet's lips quirked into a knowing smile. "Let's just say there's a tentative agreement, a promise to support the rodeo and the ranch. And it involves that nasty little condition the benefactor added to his offer. Someone here is contemplating marriage."

The table erupted in a chorus of guesses and denials. Sawyer laughed heartily. "Marriage? You mean one of us is on the chopping block? Jet, you're pulling our legs!"

Chris's voice held a flicker of skepticism. "Come on, Jet. Quit teasing us. Who's getting hitched?" He looked pointedly at each man in the room. Every head shook no.

Jet's gaze swept over the ranch hands, a mysterious look in his eyes. "I can't say just yet. But I promise you, the benefactor won't back out. But just so we cover all bases, we're going ahead with the rodeo, and we're going to make it a success."

Chris's eyes narrowed in thought, and a sly grin spread across his face. "You know, it could only be Martha or Dawn."

The table fell into an intrigued silence, the possibilities swirling in their minds.

"Martha? Really?"

Debra Chapoton

Chapter 18

THE MONTANA SKY seemed hand-painted with hues of orange and gold as Jet and Dawn mounted their horses, ready for a leisurely trail ride. Jet's posture exuded confidence, a testament to the progress he'd made with his riding skills, thanks to Chris. Dawn, this time more at ease atop her horse, met his gaze with an excited smile. "So, cowboy, where are we heading?"

With a confident grin, Jet clucked at his horse and said, "Dawn, get ready for a ride that's sure to *stirrup* some fun!"

"What? We're going to do puns? Hmm, I'm going to have to challenge you on that."

Jet's lips curled into a mischievous grin. "Challenge accepted, ma'am. Now ... I thought we'd mosey on over to a grassy spot by the lake. I reckon it's the perfect place for a picnic. Martha packed us some sandwiches and fruit."

Dawn's eyes glinted. "A picnic, huh? Sandwiches and fruit? I'm sure it'll be so *berry* delicious, positively un-*'fig'*-ettable!"

Jet's laugh echoed and his horse's ears twitched repeatedly.

As they rode side by side, their conversation became a lively exchange of puns, wordplay, and shared laughter. They spoke of horses and rodeos, ranch life and Montana.

As they trotted along the trail, Jet grew quiet. Dawn turned to him and quipped, "Boy, Jet, you really know how to *rein* in a good conversation."

He had no come-back but a smile.

Sunlight flitted between the leaves, dappling their path. Eventually, they reached the tranquil spot Jet had mentioned, the small lake shimmering in the sunlight. After tethering their horses, he spread out a blanket and revealed a picnic spread with much more than sandwiches and fruit. Their laughter continued as they sat on a rock, savoring the simple pleasure of a meal shared in good company.

Dawn's gaze met Jet's, her smile flirtatious. "You know, Mr. Armstrong, you've certainly outdone yourself with this picnic. Are you trying to impress me, the cook?"

Jet's grin matched hers, his voice filled with mock humility. "Well, ma'am, I can't say I'm *not* tryin' to make a good impression."

Dessert was eaten on paper plates with plastic forks. Dawn playfully tapped her fork against Jet's plate, and said, "Jet, your dessert looks so amazing, it's *'muffin'* short of a masterpiece. Mind if I *'pie'*-jack a bite?"

"Of course. It's store-bought, though. And can't compare to the desserts you make."

As they chatted, the chemistry between them crackled like the energy in the air before a summer storm. Jet's heart raced, and he leaned in, wanting to bridge the gap between them with a kiss. The flat-topped boulder they sat upon was high enough to mimic a small loveseat, but she had sat down first and he'd had to sit on her right with his prosthetic next to her. To kiss her would require an awkward twist he was more than willing to risk, but a number of thoughts flooded his brain. As the moment hung in the air, he pulled back, a conflict warring within him.

"Jet, is everything okay?"

He tried to keep his expression unreadable as a cloud of doubt passed over his eyes. "Dawn, there's something I need to tell you. But I can't tell you just yet."

Their moment of intimacy was replaced by an awkward silence. The atmosphere grew heavy with the strain of unspoken words, and their once-flirtatious conversation transformed into stilted exchanges, the humor gone. He'd ruined it. He'd ruined his chance to be honest.

She said something about Corey.

He told her Chris had helped him with riding.

She said Martha was worried about Duke getting old.

He said something about the weather.

The mood was lost.

When Dawn mentioned the lawsuit, Jet's mood shifted further. He withdrew completely, his answers becoming monosyllabic. The remainder of the picnic felt tense, and as they mounted their horses to return to the ranch, their silence was a stark contrast to the earlier vibrant conversation.

The trail ride back to the ranch felt longer than before, casting a lethal shadow over the connection they'd built.

Chapter 19

SEATED IN DR. LANGDON'S office, Jet's gaze fixated on a point on the wall, his voice laden with apprehension. "Doc, I can't tell Dawn the truth. Not about the ranch, the benefactor, or any of it."

Dr. Langdon leaned in, his expression thoughtful. "Jet, I understand your concerns, but keeping these secrets will affect your relationship with Dawn."

Jet's jaw tightened, a flicker of pain crossing his eyes. "You don't understand, Doc. I've been down that road before. My past relationship, the engagement ... it didn't end well. I can't bear the thought of going through that kind of loss again."

Dr. Langdon's gaze softened as he observed Jet's turmoil. "Jet, I sense that your connection with Dawn is stronger than you're willing to admit. Keeping secrets won't protect you from heartache."

Jet's fingers clenched into fists, his voice almost a whisper. "It's not just about protecting myself. I don't want to be the cause of any pain for Dawn."

Dr. Langdon adjusted his position, his expression contemplative. "Jet, let me propose a different perspective. What if I told you that revealing the truth could strengthen your bond with Dawn? Honesty, even when it's difficult, can build trust."

Jet's brows nearly met together, skepticism in his eyes. "How do you figure?"

"Think about it. If Dawn finds out about your secrets from someone else or stumbles upon them herself, she might feel hurt, betrayed even. But if you're the one to open up to her, to let her into your world, it shows vulnerability and sincerity."

Jet's features softened as he considered the idea. "I just ... I can't bear the thought of her looking at me differently."

"Jet, you're not defined by your past mistakes or your secrets. You're defined by your actions in the present. If you're honest with Dawn, it shows your commitment to a future built on trust."

Jet sighed, a blend of apprehension and hope in his eyes. "But what if she can't forgive me? What if she walks away?"

"And she might walk away if you don't tell her. You won't know until you try. And if she's as understanding and caring as you believe her to be, she might surprise you."

Jet's fingers fidgeted with the edge of the armchair. "My fiancée promised she'd wait for me while I was deployed, but when I came back without my leg… she found excuses to leave. I felt abandoned, broken."

"And now you fear causing Dawn the same pain?"

Jet nodded, his throat tight with emotions. "Dawn is different. I've never felt this kind of connection before. I can't bear the thought of losing her because of my lies."

"Jet, what if there's a way to bridge the gap between truth and trust? A way to reveal your past, your intentions, without risking everything. Without even talking to her."

Jet's brows rose. "How?"

Dr. Langdon's eyes were unwavering. "You've been working on yourself, Jet, confronting your past and your fears. You've come a long way, and it's time to put that progress to the test. What if you write a letter to Dawn, one where you lay your cards on the table?"

Jet blinked, the idea both daunting and intriguing. "A letter?"

Dr. Langdon dipped his head. "Yes. In this letter, you can tell Dawn about your past, your fears, and your reasons for keeping the truth hidden. Explain how much she means to you, and that you want to be honest moving forward. Give her the choice to decide if she wants to continue this journey with you."

Jet's mind buzzed with thoughts, the idea both appealing and nerve-wracking. "But what if she reads the letter and decides she can't trust me anymore?"

"If your connection is as strong as you believe, she'll appreciate your honesty. And if she decides to give you a chance, it will be built on a foundation of trust. Sometimes, taking a leap of faith is the only way to move forward."

Chapter 20

THE AROMA OF Dawn's mouthwatering lasagna filled the air as the ranch hands gathered in the dining room, ready to indulge. Laughter and camaraderie flowed, creating a warm atmosphere as they exchanged stories of the day's work. Suddenly, the door swung open, and Martha entered with a look of astonishment written across her features. She was wearing a nice dress, adorned with a string of pearls that embodied her understated grace, but the ensemble was something she'd wear to church and not around the ranch.

Breaking through the lively chatter, Martha's voice rang out, her expression one of disbelief and triumph. "Listen to this, cowboys! I've got news that'll knock your boots off!"

The room fell into a hushed silence as the boys turned their attention to Martha, their plates momentarily forgotten. Martha took a deep breath, her eyes alight with excitement. "I've just returned from town. The government had a change of heart. There's no plan for the new highway, after all. The whole thing's been scrapped. The ranch is safe, and we don't need to worry about raising funds or fulfilling any marriage conditions!"

Cheers erupted throughout the room, a chorus of jubilation that filled the space with contagious elation, punctuated by whoops of delight. The ranch hands exchanged triumphant looks, their disbelief mirrored in their expressions.

Chris raised a skeptical eyebrow. "Don't we still need to worry about paying the lawyers?"

Martha's brows spiked upward. "You won't believe this, but the lawyers said their fees were already taken care of. I can't make heads or tails of it!"

The room erupted into more cheers, the tension of the impending court battle lifting like a heavy fog. Jet's eyes shined as he glanced around at his fellow ranch hands. "Well, now that's something to celebrate!" He leaned back in his chair, a satisfied smile on his face. "Looks like luck's finally turned our way."

"It's not luck," Martha said, "it's prayers answered."

Sawyer raised a toast with his glass. "To unexpected blessings and a ranch saved!"

With a grin, Jet turned to Martha. "How 'bout we still have that rodeo? Not for the money, but just for the fun of it and to spread the word about this place."

Martha's smile matched Jet's enthusiasm. "You've got yourself a deal, Jet. But here's the twist—I still want the money ... but ... all the money raised should be split among you hardworking ranch hands."

Dawn lingered by the open door, her gaze fixed on Jet's face. She couldn't help but wonder if he felt the same jumble of emotions she did—relief, yes, but also a heap of disappointment at the sudden shift in circumstances. There was no need for that marriage pact anymore. Their eyes met for a fleeting moment. Though their picnic had ended strangely, she still felt overwhelmingly attracted to him.

The ranch hands continued to celebrate and laughter filled the room. Dawn was quietly lost in thought, wondering about the path that had been diverted, this unexpected turn. Yes, prayers were answered, but …

She caught Jet's gaze again through the open door, a soft smile playing on his lips. She watched him, wondering—hoping really—if he shared her conflicted feelings about the sudden change of plans.

Tangled in Fate's Reins

Chapter 21

AFTER HER KITCHEN duties ended—with the help of Corey whose youthful energy and constant singing or humming started to wear thin—Dawn retreated to her room, the events of the day swirling in her mind like leaves caught in a tornado. She perched on the edge of her bed, her thoughts a tumultuous blend of gratitude, uncertainty, and regret. Just as she wrestled with her emotions, an envelope slid under her door, catching her attention. She stared at it for several moments. Her heart quickened as she moved to pick it up. It wasn't regular mail. No address. No stamp. She flung open the door, but whoever had slipped it under the door was gone.

She opened the envelope and pulled out the letter, turned it over to see that Jet had signed it, and then began to read:

Dear Dawn,

I hope you can read my writing. There are things I need to share with you, things I should have shared long before now. Things I haven't been able to say out loud.

Dawn's pulse quickened as she absorbed Jet's words, her thoughts racing alongside the ink on the page. His honesty was a raw current that flowed through her, stirring emotions she'd held back.

I used my trust fund, (yes, I have one) to engage the lawyers for the ranch. I became the anonymous benefactor, a role I played in secret. The marriage condition I added to the donation was a spur-of-the-moment idea. I thought it might inspire excitement among the guys, never dreaming it would be taken seriously. Or that I'd make a sort-of proposal to you. That pact. Honestly, I wasn't trying to deceive you. I mean that.

Dawn's breath caught in her throat as Jet's revelations unfurled before her.

I wasn't completely honest with you, and for that, I'm deeply sorry. But I have no regrets about getting to know you better. You've shown me a world of warmth and understanding, qualities I value more than words can say.

Tears welled in Dawn's eyes as Jet's sincerity reached out to her through the ink on the page, but mostly she was sad because she feared to read on. Was he going to apologize for leading her on? Was he writing this to get out of any kind of romantic future?

I hope, Dawn, that we can still be friends, oh, no, there it was: he only wanted to be friends, *that you can find it in your heart to trust me despite my omissions. And though I've struggled with doubts, I've come to believe that no one would want to be tied to half a man like me.*

Dawn's fingers trembled as she reached the final lines of the letter, a soft sob escaping her lips. The weight of Jet's self-doubt was a heavy burden she longed to alleviate. But it sounded like he didn't want to pursue her at all.

Tangled in Fate's Reins

She reread the last line. *I've come to believe that no one would want to be tied to half a man like me.*

That wasn't true. *She* wanted to be with him.

With the letter clutched in her hand, Dawn rose from the bed, a sure decision sparking in her heart. She knew what she had to do. As she stepped into the hallway, the silent echo of Jet's words accompanied her, propelling her forward. The letter was incomplete. He hadn't said the final words. He hadn't said the pact was off.

The night air whispered doubts in her ears as she made her way through the ranch; she hesitated in the hall, again at the door, then went out onto the porch. Each hesitation was a declaration of her own vulnerability, a fear that the bond growing between them had all been in her imagination.

In the soft glow of the moonlight, Dawn spotted Jet standing by the stables, a figure of strength and of weakness. She walked toward him.

Debra Chapoton

Chapter 22

THE BARN WAS bathed in the gentle glow of lantern light, casting soft shadows on the rough-hewn walls. Dawn's heart raced as she approached Jet, her steps hesitant but resolute. He turned. His stormy blue eyes held the depth of his past struggles and his unyielding resolve.

"Dawn," he breathed, his voice a whispered exhalation.

"I read your letter," she began, her voice barely more than a tremor. "I've come to find you."

Jet's gaze held hers. "I meant every word. I never wanted to deceive you."

Dawn lowered her chin, her eyes shimmering with unshed tears. "I know, Jet. I understand why you did what you did. If you meant the letter to push me away … it's not going to work."

Silence hung between them. Unspoken words and unvoiced feelings readily translated by hungry hearts. Then, Jet took a step closer, his fingers brushing against hers in a tentative caress.

"Dawn, these past weeks have been like becoming whole again. You've made me feel complete." His voice trembled, and he continued, "And I've realized that my heart ... it's been waiting for you."

Dawn's breath caught, her heart pounding in her chest. "Jet, I never expected to find love here, in this place. But ... my heart ... it's been waiting for you too."

The admission hung in the air, a bridge connecting their souls as the world around them seemed to fade into insignificance. Jet took a step closer, his gaze locked on hers, his voice steady and unwavering.

"I don't have a ring, and I can't get down on one knee, but I can't wait any longer." He paused, his voice husky with emotion. "Will you marry me? For real."

Dawn's heart soared, her eyes glistening with tears of joy. "Yes, Jet."

He let out a breath he hadn't realized he'd been holding, a smile breaking across his face. "I promise to make it up to you with a proper proposal, and a ring ... any ring you want."

Amid the sounds of nickering horses and the rustle of hay, Jet looked into Dawn's eyes and asked, "In the meantime ... will you wear this, as a promise of the love we've found?" He put two fingers on the silver chain around his neck and pulled up his dog tags.

Tears of happiness spilled down Dawn's cheeks as she extended her hand, her voice full of emotion. "Yes, Jet, I will."

And then, as if guided by an invisible force, their lips met in a kiss that was both sweet and passionate, sealing their commitment to each other and promising a journey that would last a lifetime.

Tangled in Fate's Reins

THE END

Want more?
Oh, you didn't think I'd leave it there, did you? Book 2, RODEO ROMANCE, continues the *Hearts Unbridled* series at the Double Horseshoe Ranch with Corey's story. You'll still find out how Jet and Dawn's romance progresses while watching Corey develop feelings for one of the competitors in the ranch's rodeo. Find book 2, RODEO ROMANCE, only on Amazon.

Follow me for new book releases:
https://www.amazon.com/stores/author/B003MX4NCS

MORE BOOKS by this author writing under the pen names of Debra Chapoton, Boone Patchard, or Marlisa Kriscott:

Cowboy Romance:
TANGLED IN FATE'S REINS
RODEO ROMANCE
A COWBOY'S PROMISE
HEARTSTRINGS AND HORSESHOES
KISSES AT SUNDOWN

Scottish Romance:
THE HIGHLANDER'S SECRET PRINCESS
THE HIGHLANDER'S ENGLISH MAIDEN
THE HIGHLANDER'S HIDDEN CASTLE
THE HIGHLANDER'S HEART OF STONE
THE HIGHLANDER'S FORBIDDEN LOVE

SECOND CHANCE TEACHER ROMANCE – Christian romance series written under the pen name Marlisa Kriscott:
AARON AFTER SCHOOL
SONIA'S SECRET SOMEONE
MELANIE'S MATCH
SCHOOL'S OUT
SUMMER SCHOOL
THE SPANISH TUTOR
A NOVEL THING

Young Adult Novels:
EDGE OF ESCAPE Psychological Thriller - Innocent adoration escalates to stalking and abduction in this psychological thriller. SOMMERFALLE is the German version of EDGE OF ESCAPE

THE GUARDIAN'S DIARY Young Adult Coming of Age - Jedidiah, a 17-year-old champion skateboarder with a defect he's been hiding all of his life, must risk exposure to rescue a girl that's gone missing.

SHELTERED Young Adult Paranormal - Ben, a high school junior, has found a unique way to help homeless teens, but he must first bring the group together to fight against supernatural forces.

A SOUL'S KISS Young Adult Paranormal - When a tragic accident leaves Jessica comatose, her spirit escapes her body. Navigating a supernatural realm is tough, but being half dead has its advantages. Like getting into people's thoughts. Like taking over someone's body. Like experiencing romance on a whole new plane - literally.

EXODIA Dystopian Biblical Retelling - By 2093 American life is a strange mix of failing technologies, psychic predictions, and radiation induced abilities. Tattoos are mandatory to differentiate two classes, privileged and slave. Dalton Battista fears that his fading tattoo is a deadly omen. He's either the heir of the brutal tyrant of the new capital city, Exodia or he's its prophesied redeemer.

OUT OF EXODIA In this sequel to EXODIA, Dalton Battista takes on his prophesied identity as Bram O'Shea. When this psychic teen leads a city of 21st century American survivalists out from under an oppressive regime, he puts the escape plan at risk by trusting the mysterious god-like David Ronel.

THE GIRL IN THE TIME MACHINE Young Adult Time Travel - A desperate teen with a faulty time machine. What could go wrong? 17-year-old Laken is torn between revenge and righting a wrong. Sci-Fi suspense.

THE TIME BENDER Young Adult Alien Sci-Fi - A stolen kiss could put the universe at risk. Selina doesn't think Marcum's spaceship is anything more than one heck of a science project … until he takes her to the moon and back.

THE TIME PACER Young Adult Alien Sci-Fi - Alex discovered he was half-alien right after he learned how to manipulate time. Now he has to fight the star cannibals, fly a space ship, work on his relationship with Selina, and stay clear of Coreg, full-blooded alien rival and possible galactic traitor. Once they reach their ancestral planet all three are plunged into a society where schooling is more than indoctrination

THE TIME STOPPER Young Adult Alien Sci-Fi - Young recruit Marcum learns battle-craft, infiltration and multiple languages at the Interstellar Combat Academy. He and his arch rival Coreg jeopardize their futures by exceeding the space travel limits and flying to Earth in search of a time-bender. They find Selina whose ability to slow the passage of time will be invaluable in fighting other aliens. But Marcum loses his heart to her and when Coreg takes her twenty light years away he remains on Earth in order to develop a far greater talent than time-bending. Now he's ready to return home and get the girl.

THE TIME ENDER Young Adult Alien Sci-Fi - Selina Langston is confused about recurring feelings for the wrong guy/alien. She's pretty sure Alex is her soulmate and Coreg should not be trusted at all. But Marcum … well, when he returns to Klaqin and rescues her she begins to see him in a different light.

TO DIE UPON A KISS Gender-swapped Retelling of *Othello* - Several teenagers' lives intertwine during one eventful week full of love, betrayal and murder in this futuristic, gender-swapped retelling of Shakespeare's Othello.

Tangled in Fate's Reins

HERE WITHOUT A TRACE Young Adult Parallel World - Hailey and Logan enter a parallel world through hypnosis in order to rescue a girl gone missing.

LOVE CONTAINED Christian Suspense - Trapped in a shipping container, sinking to the depths of the ocean … but this isn't the worst thing that's happened to Henry … or Max.

SPELL OF THE SHADOW DRAGON Epic Sci-Fi Fantasy - Four hundred years after colonizing a planet ruled by dragons, the future of the human race hangs in the balance once again.

CURSE OF THE WINTER DRAGON – Epic Sci-Fi Fantasy – Sequel to SPELL OF THE SHADOW DRAGON

A FAULT OF GRAVES – young adult thriller - A disastrous fall into the depths of our planet turns into a desperate fight for survival.

Non-fiction:
35 LESSONS IN THE PSALMS Ready to use Sunday School lessons and/or personal Bible Study Workbook

PRAYER JOURNAL AND BIBLE STUDY FOR MEN

PRAYER JOURNAL AND BIBLE STUDY (for women)

GUIDED PRAYER JOURNAL FOR WOMEN

Debra Chapoton

OLD TESTAMENT LESSONS IN THE BIBLE
Sunday School lessons and/or personal Bible study

NEW TESTAMENT LESSONS IN THE BIBLE
Sunday School lessons and/or personal Bible study

TEENS IN THE BIBLE Sunday School lessons and/or personal Bible study

MOMS IN THE BIBLE Sunday School lessons and/or personal Bible study

ANIMALS IN THE BIBLE Sunday School lessons and/or personal Bible study

PRAYER JOURNAL AND BIBLE STUDY IN THE GOSPELS

HOW TO BLEND FAMILIES This guide gives step by step advice from experienced educators and also provides several fill-in worksheets to help you resolve family relationships, deal with discipline, navigate the financials, and create a balanced family with happy people.

BUILDING BIG PINE LODGE A journal of our experiences building a full log home

CROSSING THE SCRIPTURES A Bible Study supplement for studying each of the 66 books of the Old and New Testaments.

Tangled in Fate's Reins

300 PLUS TEACHER HACKS and TIPS A guide for teachers at all levels of experience with hacks, tricks, and tips to help you get and give the most out of teaching.

HOW TO HELP YOUR CHILD SUCCEED IN SCHOOL A guide for parents to motivate, encourage and propel their kids to the head of the class. Includes proven strategies and tips from teachers.

HOW TO TEACH A FOREIGN LANGUAGE Tips, advice, and resources for foreign language teachers and student teachers.

200 Creative Writing Prompts Workbook

400 Creative Writing Prompts Workbook

Advanced Creative Writing Prompts Workbook

Beyond Creative Writing Prompts

BRAIN POWER PUZZLES Volume 1
Stretch yourself by solving anagrams, word searches, cryptograms, mazes, math puzzles, Sudoku, crosswords, daisy puzzles, boggle boards, pictograms, riddles, and more in these entertaining puzzles books.

BRAIN POWER PUZZLES Volume 2
BRAIN POWER PUZZLES Volume 3
BRAIN POWER PUZZLES Volume 4
BRAIN POWER PUZZLES Volume 5 (Spanish Student Edition)

Debra Chapoton

BRAIN POWER PUZZLES Volume 6 (Math Edition)
BRAIN POWER PUZZLES Volume 7
BRAIN POWER PUZZLES Volume 8 (Bible Theme)
BRAIN POWER PUZZLES Volume 9
BRAIN POWER PUZZLES Volume 10 (Christmas Edition)
BRAIN POWER PUZZLES Volume 11 (Word Search Challenge)

Children's books:

THE SECRET IN THE HIDDEN CAVE 12-year-old Missy Stark and her new friend Kevin Jackson discover dangerous secrets when they explore the old lodge, the woods, the cemetery, and the dark caves beneath the lake. They must solve the riddles and follow the clues to save the old lodge from destruction.

MYSTERY'S GRAVE After Missy and Kevin solved THE SECRET IN THE HIDDEN CAVE, they thought the rest of the summer at Big Pine Lodge would be normal. But there are plenty of surprises awaiting them in the woods, the caves, the stables, the attic and the cemetery. Two new families arrive and one family isn't human.

BULLIES AND BEARS In their latest adventure at Big Pine Lodge, Missy and Kevin discover more secrets in the caves, the attic, the cemetery and the settlers' ruins. They have to stay one step ahead of four teenage bullies, too, as well as three hungry bears. This summer's escapades become more and more challenging for these two twelve-year-olds. How will they make it through another week?

Tangled in Fate's Reins

A TICK IN TIME 12-year-old Tommy MacArthur plunges into another dimension thanks to a magical grandfather clock. Now he must find his way through a strange land, avoid the danger lurking around every corner, and get back home. When he succeeds, he dares his new friend Noelle to return with him, but who and what follows them back means more trouble and more adventure.

BIGFOOT DAY, NINJA NIGHT When 12-year-old Anna skips the school fair to explore the woods with Callie, Sydney, Austin, and Natalie, they find evidence of Bigfoot. No way! It looks like his tracks are following them. But that's not the worst part. And neither is stumbling upon Bigfoot's shelter. The worst part is they get separated and now they can't find Callie or the path that leads back to the school.

In the second story Luke and his brother, Nick, go on a boys-only camping trip, but things get weird and scary very quickly. Is there a ninja in the woods with them? Mysterious things happen as day turns into night.

THE TUNNEL SERIES 12-year-old Nick escapes from a reformatory but gets side-tracked traveling through multiple tunnels, each with a strange destination. He must find his way home despite barriers like invisibility. When he teams up with Samantha they begin to uncover the secret to all the tunnels. (6 books in series)

Early Readers
THE KINDNESS PARADE, THE CARING KIDS: SPREADING KINDNESS EVERYWHERE

Debra Chapoton

THE COLORS OF FRIENDSHIP: THE CARING KIDS, EMBRACING DIVERSITY
BELIEVE IN YOURSELF, THE CARING KIDS: BUILDING SELF ESTEEM
FRIENDS WITH FUR AND FEATHERS: THE CARING KIDS, ANIMAL FRIENDS
CELEBRATIONS ALL YEAR ROUND: THE CARING KIDS: OUR SPECIAL DAYS
FEELINGS IN FULL COLOR: THE CARING KIDS: A GUIDE TO FEELINGS
THE CARING KIDS complete series

Follow me for new book releases:
https://www.amazon.com/stores/author/B003MX4NCS

Made in the USA
Middletown, DE
06 July 2024